TICKLED HARD

Adam Small

TICKLED HARD

Writing copyright © 2014 Adam Small

This book is copyright © 2014 Adam Small

All Rights Reserved.

In grateful memory of "Jack," whose contributions to the male foot fetish and tickling community far exceeded what he ever lived to see.

May he be at peace wherever he is.

ADULT CONTENT WARNING

For mature readers only. All characters in this novella involved in explicit acts are at least 18 years of age. While there is no sex in this novella, it does contain graphic descriptions catering to those with a male bondage, tickling, and foot fetish.

All characters engaged in graphic acts are at least partially clothed in all scenes. This book will be enjoyable for gay men, straight men, and straight women with an appreciation for male feet, bondage, and tickling.

Still, your author asks that only those readers who are at least 18 years of age and who are legally allowed to view such material read this book.

Thank you.

Adam Small

CHAPTER 1

I sit straight up in the bed, my strong body covered in a thin layer of glistening sweat. I look around, my heart pounding, my chest heaving. All I see is the light from the streetlamp outside my window forcing its way through the crevices in the blinds.

I had the same dream. Again.

Almost by instinct, my fingers make their way down my lightly hairy legs to the part of my body where the hair ends and the smooth flesh of a very young man's ankles begins. I reach past the ankle and fumble with my toes before returning my hands to my ankles, wrapping my fingers around them. I watch my fingers, like chains, around my ankles as they grasp tighter and tighter. I know what I want. I've wanted it for years.

For a moment my fingers, whose knuckles must surely have turned white from so tightly grasping my bare ankles, let go. I look over at the mirror, and I realize the faint light that makes its way into my room from the same streetlamp allows me to see my own features. A boy had lain in this bed since he was old enough to lie in a bed alone. Now, I stare at a man, and a man stares back.

Perhaps I'm not *really* a man though. Not yet. After all, it's only been two days since my eighteenth birthday. If nothing else, though, the law makes me a man. And that's important. Now that I'm 18, I have a critical task ahead of me.

My fingers once again reach down to my ankles and wrap around them. My ankles are thin enough that my third finger reaches my thumb with just a little stretching. I imagine my fingers really *are* chains. Or rope, perhaps. I imagine what it would feel like if I didn't have the power I exercised a moment ago when I let go of my own ankles. I wonder what it would feel like to be completely out of control, my bare soles helpless to the delightful tortures my master would want to inflict on them. So far, he hasn't touched me. And it has been my youth that prevented it. My youth and threats from my father. Maybe my master really is very moral. Or very legal. Or very afraid of my old man. But now none of these virtues or fears come into play. Now he can do as he pleases. Now I can become the willing slave I've always wanted to be.

If he will have me.

Jason. Damn, what a hot name.

I'm naked except for a pair of boxer briefs I left on the night before. I work out, but not much. My chest is toned, but it's not a truly muscular chest. I have short, dark brown hair. My arms are toned, as well, but I wouldn't exactly call them cut arms. I look over at my chest and my arms in the mirror as I sit up in the bed, my eyes still wide from the exhilaration of the dream.

In my dream, Jason had me tied down. In what position, I don't know. I only know that my master had "forced" me in tight restraints and had stood in front of my bare feet, staring at them with a sexy, evil grin on his face.

"I'm gonna tickle the shit out of you, Michael," he told me. In my dream, I grinned back. Having Jason tickle the shit out of me is all I've ever wanted. In my dream, he reached forward with his fingers flexed like cruel claws that would crawl over my flesh, make me squirm and scream with laughter.

Then I woke up. Too soon. Now all I have by which to remember that dream is my own hands wrapped tightly around my ankles and the ghost of a memory of Jason – a man I haven't seen in nearly three years. But that's soon to change. I owe Jason a visit now that I'm a man. Will my father protest? He might. But what can he do now? Legally I'm an adult. Legally, he can't punish me. No one can.

But my master can punish me because I'll let him. He can do whatever he wants. I'll obey. Without question.

I now think back to how I met Jason. I was probably about 13 or 14, and he was a next door neighbor. He still is. I was sneaking around the back of his house acting stupid, and I smelled the weed. He flung the door open, and I knew I was caught. I half expected him to beat the shit out of me.

"You wanna try some, kid?" he asked. I froze. For a moment, I was silent. But I quickly gained just enough courage to respond.

"Sure."

I walked into his house, and Jason taught me everything from how to roll a blunt to how to inhale and how to hold the smoke in my lungs just long enough. But not too long. He said I never got very good at that, and I realized he was right the first few times I smoked with him. The coughing stopped soon after I got used to it, but I never stopped smoking too fast.

Until I stopped smoking at all. I clench my eyes in pain thinking about the day that happened. It was Dad's fault. Even now, I know I might never forgive him.

Dad is a psychologist. Mom's a surgeon, so she's never home. She's home so rarely, in fact, I feel I barely know her. Dad's the one who raised me, if you can call it that. I wouldn't.

I open my eyes and see the faint light shining on my knuckles, which have turned white again as I grasp my bare ankles even tighter. I let up a little, and I think maybe I'm being too hard on my old man. He hasn't been the most loving, emotionally available father, but whose father is? He's definitely competent and professional. Like an attorney or a stockbroker. I'll probably miss him when he dies like I'd miss my banker.

So yes, he's a psychologist, and his whole life is psychology. It seems all he does is psychoanalyze everyone and everything. He diagnoses people he sees on the news. Everyone from the latest psychopath serial killer to the president. As this comes to my mind, I laugh. Loud.

"What's wrong?" my dad hollers from the other room, banging on the wall. My dad has the ears of a bat. It seems nothing ever gets past him. He's heard things like mice squeaking across the floor or the hum of an engine miles away that I couldn't make out. I'm perpetually amazed at the things he can hear. Sometimes I jokingly say I'm surprised he didn't hear the fumes coming off all the pot I smoked with Jason for a few years as a younger teen. To my knowledge, he never found out about that. What he did find out about, however, was enough to wreck a lot of relationships and startle, if not terrify, a lot of people.

"Nothing," I call back. I grasp my ankles hard again and flex my toes. I imagine even now my feet would look so young and soft to a man like Jason, who turned 30 a year or so ago. Vulnerable maybe. I wonder if he'll like that when he inevitably sees them. My vulnerable feet.

I'm actually not at all sure what he'll think of them when we meet. I wonder if he'll still like them. And me. If I'll still freak him out. If he'll want to talk to me. I wonder how much he's changed since my last horrible experience with him.

I let go of my ankles and lie back down, staring up at the ceiling, listening to the sounds of night coming in from outside. I move my hands over my head and imagine Jason has tied them there. Having just turned 18 and never having experienced such bondage myself, you must wonder how I know so much about the various bondage positions. Rest assured, I know them all. But knowing them is not enough. I want to experience them.

As I lie here, I spread my legs so my feet lie at each corner of the bed. I stretch my arms out to the side. This is called spread eagle. At least it would be if there were rope around my wrists and ankles. It's the most comfortable bondage position I'm aware of. The easiest, but will leave a young man like me devilishly vulnerable to Jason's cruel fingers. I smile. Then I laugh again, but this time softer, ensuring I won't disturb my asshole dad. I throw my head back and laugh as loud as I can without doing so. I imagine Jason's unmerciful fingers going over my whole body, tickling me without letting up in the slightest. I flex my toes and imagine Jason attacking the soft, pink soles of my young, bare feet. I imagine him running his fingers over them, showing less and less mercy the more I laugh and beg. I imagine the rope binding my bare feet for my own ticklish torture and his ticklish pleasure.

I know Jason wants this as much as I do. As I said, he's never touched me. But he wants it. He wants it bad.

Now I close my eyes but keep my submissive, pseudo-bondage position as I imagine Jason straddling me on my bed. I open my eyes and see he's not there, so I close them again. I want to make this fantasy as real as possible. I imagine Jason taking his fingers and digging into my young armpits. Again, I throw back my head and laugh, but softly. I laugh till the salty tears start stinging my eyes. My fantasy master has no mercy on his boy. He tickles me like I'm his prey, his slave, his property. And I want nothing more than to be Jason's property. He had the best pot when I was a kid. Now that I'm a man, he'll have the best bondage and tickle torture. I lick my lips in anticipation of what's surely to come.

Except... what if it doesn't?

I open my eyes again and put my hands down at my side, still breathless from the fantasy I explored in the realms of my own mind. I pull down my boxer briefs and grab my cock, gently starting to stroke before moving my hand over it harder and harder, faster and faster. I'm fucking my hand with my cock full force now, and it's throbbing. All I'm thinking about is how badly I want Jason to tickle the shit out of me and make me suffer like his tickle slaveboy. He had that opportunity once and turned it down. Now I'm 18. I'm legal. I pray to whatever gods will listen that he doesn't turn me down again.

My eyes are wide open now, and I feel the sweat still covering my body. I'm especially aware of it on my forehead as it forms tiny beads and starts dripping down my face. My cock is hard as a fucking rock. I'm getting close. I close my eyes again and imagine Jason torturing my young, soft feet with his fingers. Or maybe this time he uses the prongs of a fork as he tickles me. No mercy. I'm a man now. A tickle slave. No mercy for a tickle slave like me.

I'm moaning now, and I hope my dad doesn't hear. Why he chooses to sleep in the room right next to mine remains a mystery. Maybe he feels it's his parental duty to at least try to spy on me. Or maybe he didn't give it that much thought at all. All I know is that I'm moaning, and thoughts of Jason and his fingers or other instruments of tickle torture attacking me consume my mind as I get closer and closer to shooting my hot, sticky load all over myself. Maybe this time I'll hit my face. My cum may just shoot to my nipples. I never know. It depends on how horny I am at the time I happen to be getting off. Right now, I'm horny as fuck. And that's probably because I know I'm going to confront Jason for the first time in years. Now is my opportunity.

I shoot my load all over myself. I enter a state of ecstasy no man can describe but every man has felt. As I finish, realizing there's a little jizz on my cheek, I lie on the bed panting, now listening to Dad's snoring in the next room. So much for keeping him up with my fantasy.

I wipe my cum on the sheet, adding to no telling how much is already there. Then I roll over and try to get a few more hours' rest before I wake up and go see Jason. For the first time in years. Maybe I can convince him to do the things I failed to convince him to do before. I want that so bad. More than anything.

CHAPTER 2

I wake up again, but this time not in the panic I did last night. The light of the rising sun replaces the light of the streetlamp as it makes its way in through the closed blinds. My body, covered in sweat the night before, now lies dry on the sheets beneath me as my eyes start to open and I take in the new day. And as they do, I remember the dream, the bondage, the tickling, Jason.

Jason.

Yes, he still consumes my thoughts, even now. And even now, I still long to see him. I turned 18 a few days ago, but it's taken until today for me to gain the courage to make my way to his house after a few years away from him. At least the courage to knock on his door. After all, I did try yesterday. But today I will find a new courage. Today, I will go and see him. Today, I will confront my greatest fear. Two of them really.

First, I will confront my fear that Jason will reject me after all that happened a few years ago. Second, I'll confront my fear of my dad, who all but swore it would be a cold day in hell before he'd allow me to see Jason again. But what can he do now? I'm 18. I'm a man. Legally.

I stand up and put some shorts on over my boxer briefs, as well as a tee shirt and some brown leather flip flops. Then I make my way downstairs, and the smell of bacon grease and eggs greets me. It's a little after 6. Dad will be going into work to talk some sense into his fucked up patients in just a little while. If nothing has changed, Jason will be going to work, as well. I don't have much time.

"Morning," Dad says with a quick, cold stare before he continues his ritual of making breakfast. Since Mom is never around, he's ended up making it for years. I eye him without responding, and I sit at the table, remembering back to a happier childhood when he seemed so much nicer. "Breakfast will be ready soon."

"Thanks," I reply, "but I'm not hungry."

Dad stops for a moment, and I listen to the sizzling grease in the pan as he stands with his eyes closed in front of the stove.

"Not hungry," he repeats, almost to himself. Then he whirls around, ignoring the skillet on the hot stove. "You're a teenager, Michael. When are you not hungry?"

"I'm a man now. And not today."

"A man," my dad repeats with a laugh. Then he stops laughing. Just a little too soon. It's like he finally realizes what I'm saying.

Yes, times have changed a lot. When I was a kid, Dad played games with me, spent time with me. As a young child, he picked me up and moved me around, and I often felt like I was on a roller coaster from the way he tossed me about. It was exhilarating. A few years later, as a middle grade child, he started to tickle me. No, it was nothing weird. Not like that. He just tickled me like any father would tickle his son. It consisted of nothing more than a few light pokes here and there, maybe on my sides or the soles of my feet. But I took it as an expression of love. It was the acceptance I took from it that I don't expect now. Now, I feel such shame being around my father. Shame from what he knows about me. Shame from what I know about him. Shame in general.

But there's something about my dad's childhood tickling that haunts me. It's as if that light tickling from the only grown man in my life at the time has become a symbol of the expression of love. Even now I long for an older man to tickle me, but my dad stopped shortly after I turned 11. I can only guess by then he felt I was too old. He certainly feels that way now. Now, even a quick hug is something we reserve for the solemnest of occasions – funerals or Christmas. Times we can't really make an excuse not to touch each other.

Still, thoughts of my dad tickling me now haunt me. I wonder, even now, what it would be like to feel his fingers digging into my flesh. Perhaps these are twisted thoughts, but they consume me all the same. I can only imagine my cock growing hard as a rock as I stand licking my lips before my father while he moves his fingers over my naked ribs, causing me to squirm as he did when I was a boy. Only now there would be an element of... electricity... that wasn't there before. And as the idea of my father tickling me circles my mind, so too do thoughts of Jason's hands going over my flesh, just as I fantasized last night.

As I said, I haven't talked to Jason in years, but I've seen out him a few times. What is it about men moving past the age of 30 that makes them so much sexier than they were even in their late 20's? I've seen Jason as my dad and I drove past his house and he was out in his yard. On rare occasion I've seen him shopping at the same grocery store. He didn't speak or even look up. My dad's eyes burned into him as we walked past, but Jason was always careful. In many ways, Jason is far more intelligent than I am. If nothing else, because he's older. But also because he knows when to back off, when to move forward, when to take a chance, when not to. He knows all these things, and I'm only now starting to learn them.

I sit at the table watching my dad fumbling with the spatula as he finishes up making breakfast, obviously still holding to the idea he might be able to convince me to eat something. I kick my feet in and out of my flip flops under the table, knowing that if Jason were here, my movements would have his undivided attention. He would furtively steal glances of my young feet kicking in and out of my sparsely covering footwear as I sit at the table. That would be the whole idea! I would move my feet in and out, hoping for him to steal glances at my young, naked feet, hoping he might take me, grab me from behind, drag me to the bedroom, and tickle the shit out of me till I'm a breathless wreck on the bed. Maybe he would even tie me down. And not just spread eagle as I fantasized the night before. Bondage is a delicious smorgasbord, each piece just waiting to be sampled. As my dad brings a plate of food and sets it in front of me, ignoring the fact I told him I'm not hungry, all I can think of is how starved I am for Jason to tickle me without mercy, to make me his lifelong tickle slave.

I try to keep myself from laughing. Even I can see how insane such a thought is. Even I can see the irony that the craziest man in my dad's life as a psychologist is his own son. How can a man who has devoted his entire life to the study of psychology – even reading books about it when he's not working – have missed the obvious fact that his kid is a nut job? Or maybe he realizes it. Maybe he always has. After all, he knows all too well my desires for tickling, and I'm sure he kicks himself night and day for having tickled me as a boy. I'm sure he blames himself for having put that fetish into my head. *What a terrible father I am,* I can imagine him saying to himself. And he's not wrong. But it's too late.

I slip my bare feet back into my flip flops and stand up, leaving the hot food on the table. I have more important things to do than consume an unhealthy breakfast with a stranger I've known my whole life.

My father takes in a deep breath of air and then slowly exhales. Maybe they taught him that when he was getting his doctorate in the 80's. Maybe that's some shitty Buddhist technique he learned back then.

"Where are you going?"

I smile at him. A wry, know-it-all smile. The smile you only expect from a cocky teenage boy.

"You have to ask?"

"No," Dad says, shaking his head. "I knew you'd do this. I've known since that first night."

"Don't talk to me about that night!" I scream, balling my hands into fists at my side, my eyes ablaze with fury as the hellish thoughts of that night come rampaging back into my mind. How can I escape the terror of that night? Will it haunt me forever, even if this story has a happy ending?

Now dad is sitting down. His silence fills the room before he speaks.

"You'll have to talk about it sometime."

"Yeah?" I respond. "Well, I'm gonna talk about it today. But not with you."

"With Jason then?"

"Who else?"

"You think he's going to help you?"

"Better than you ever did."

I see the hurt in my dad's eyes. I've wounded him. I've touched a sore spot in a man who has devoted his whole life to the mental wellbeing of others. I remind him now, for perhaps the thousandth time, of his failure to do so with his own son.

My toes flex in my flip flops. I notice. My dad doesn't. There's nothing so unremarkable to him, and yet I often notice every movement of my toes, just as Jason would if he were standing here now. And soon Jason will have a firsthand look at my young, bare feet if he wants it. I'll let him do anything he desires with them. He can tickle them till the muscles in my feet and toes are squirming in spasms, even till they ache. I don't care. There's so much more to this fetish than the mere sensation of the tickle torture. It goes deep to the emotion of true connection, true bonding. Jason and I will soon experience that, assuming he's able to get past all that's happened.

I start to walk out, not even acknowledging my dad as I leave.

"You think he's going to let this go? You think he's not afraid of me anymore?"

I don't turn to face my dad. I'm still looking at the door, holding the knob with my hand. How can I respond to that? He makes a good point. For a moment, I think of all the things I could say. But instead, I just open the door and walk out, starting to make my way to my next door neighbor's house I haven't talked to in years. The dewy grass lightly tickles my feet in my flip flops as I move closer and closer, hoping I can catch him so we'll have a moment to talk before he has to go to work. It could be wonderful – or terrible. He could throw his arms around me and tell me how fucking glad he is to see me, or he could kick me out and threaten to call the cops if I ever darken his doorstep again. Either is a viable possibility. I know this well.

And yet I have to try. I have to go over and actually knock on his door this time, at least giving both myself and him a chance at some sort of reconciliation. I have to let him know I haven't forgotten about him, that I could *never* forget about him, that thoughts of him have buried themselves deep in my brain since the last time I saw him.

And I have to let him know that I want to finish what we started a few years before, a game that – at the time – was dangerous, and no longer is. Not legally anyway. He never allowed himself to get too close that day, but I know the temptation was great. If it's great today, maybe he'll call out of work and spend his free time putting me through the rigors of delicious and devilish tickle torture the likes of which I have never felt but have always wanted to feel more than anything else. And so the dewy grass tickles my feet as a prelude hopefully to the insane tickle torture to come. I can't wait. This will be fantastic – if it happens at all.

CHAPTER 3

When Jason and I were good friends during my younger teenage years, I always just walked into his house without knocking. Now I find myself standing outside under the warm rays of the sun fighting to find the courage to tap on his door. I don't have much time. I have to act fast or Jason will have to leave for work and I'll have missed my opportunity – at least for today.

I take a deep breath as I dig my toes into my flip flops beneath me and pound on the door.

"Who the hell is it?" Jason yells from inside, obviously irritated at someone disturbing him while he's trying to get his day started. Then I see him walking toward the door through the pane of the window. He acts like he's seen a ghost when he looks into my eyes. For a moment, he stops in his tracks. But just for a moment. Then he approaches the door and opens it.

Jason is absolutely as fantastic looking as I remember him. He's wearing his mechanic shirt with his name embroidered on the front. His arms are massive and masculine and sexy. His hair, like mine, is short and brown, but he's older. A sexy kind of older. Like I said, he just turned 30 a year or so ago. His eyes and his face have just enough age to make him perfect. Working in a garage or being outside has left his face with a nice tan. And from his lips hangs an unlit cigarette I'm sure he planned to smoke on his way to work.

For a moment we stand and stare at each other, and I almost feel the cigarette will fall from Jason's lips, as he's so shocked at seeing me here. But it doesn't. Even as he speaks, he leaves it hanging there for the first few words.

"Funny seeing you here, kid," he says. It's the first time in years I've heard his voice, and I nearly melt into his arms. How I long to run to him and wrap my arms around his muscular torso. But I don't. I look past him at his table where he brazenly leaves all his paraphernalia. He grins and grabs the cigarette from his mouth, placing it behind his ear.

"You think I could...?" I start to say, but my words escape me.

Jason ignores my plea for pot, an addiction I never completely lost a taste for but never indulged outside his presence. Once I was no longer able to see this man, I stopped smoking pot cold turkey, wondering what the point of it was without him.

"Your dad know you're here?" Jason asks in an icy voice. I stare into Jason's deep, blue eyes as he speaks. I have known since I realized I would come to see him that this topic would come up. How do I address it?

"Yeah," I said. "But it doesn't matter. I'm 18 now."

"Eighteen?" Jason says, almost laughing. "When did you turn 18?"

"Couple of days ago."

"Took you this long to come over and see me, huh?"

Now I'm embarrassed. Why *did* I wait? I can tell Jason I've been busy. Or I can tell him the truth that I was afraid, that I needed time to muster the courage to come to his doorstep and knock. I can also tell him I came once before and even stood in front of his door for a long time but just couldn't bring myself to let him know I was here. Now I stand in front of Jason, and I look down at my bare feet in my flip flops. As my own gaze goes to my young, soft, white feet, Jason's immediately follows.

"I..." But the words escape me yet again.

"Give me a second, kid." Jason turns around, as if doing so will give him any privacy, and pulls his phone out of his pocket. He dials a number and stands facing away from me.

"Hey John," he says. "I've had something come up. Kinda an emergency. I won't make it in." The pause eats me alive. I suspected Jason might call out, but now that he's actually doing so, it takes me a little by surprise. "You got a trainee. I've worked with him. He does okay." Another pause. "See you tomorrow, buddy."

Hearing Jason call his coworker "buddy" is as erotic to me as hearing him call me "kid." I don't know what it is, but the warm affection of this man and the way he approaches his friends is captivating. My cock jumps in my shorts, and my toes dig just a little deeper into my flip flops.

"Eighteen, huh?" Jason says as he turns back to face me. God, he's so fucking sexy, and all I want in the world is for him to grab me and tie me to his bed, tickle the shit out of me as he did in my dream only last night. But I wait. It's a touchy subject. I can't move too fast.

"Yeah," I respond, almost whispering. Jason raises an eyebrow as he stares back at me, and I look into his deep, blue eyes. Then I look past him at the pot on the table.

"How long's it been since you smoked, kid?"

"Since last time with you."

This causes Jason to crack a smile, and he motions me over to the table. I sit down and watch as he rolls a blunt. Then he lights it and inhales. He sucks it in, long and deep.

"It's good shit," Jason says, his eyes already a little bloodshot from the drug use. "Priest has the best."

"You've always said that."

Jason leans forward. "He does. And don't start with me."

"I wasn't." I say, eyeing the blunt in Jason's fingers, licking my lips in anticipation of that pot coursing through my body. "I don't care who he is."

Jason doesn't know it, but I've actually done some research. I found out through some friends at school – back when I was in school – exactly who Priest is and where he lives. I could have gone over there a thousand times. I've got other connections besides Jason, and I could have easily convinced the little man to sell me his shit. But I didn't. To me, smoking pot is a sacred act. I would only ever do it with Jason. Still, Jason takes Priest's real identity seriously, and apparently as long as pot and anything else Priest sells remain illegal, that will be the case.

Jason extends his hand and gives me the blunt. "Slowly," he says. I take it from him and put it to my lips, inhaling as slowly as I can. I cough, but just for a moment. After a few years' break, this will take some getting used to again. But probably not as long as before.

"You wore flip flops, kid," he finally says as he watches me get high.

"Yeah."

"You never change, do you?"

"Nope."

"Flip flops all summer."

Jason is fishing. We never directly discussed his fetish for handsome, young feet. Oh, we came close once, but even he wasn't willing to go that far. Not with a 15-year-old. I know he wanted to bad at that time, but he wouldn't dare. Like I said, now he's fishing. I'm fishing, too.

"You still got that rope," I ask, taking another hit.

"Slowly," Jason says, leaning forward again and putting his hands onto mine to ease the blunt away from my lips. I look at him, and his face is so sexy. It's a dream. I nearly fall forward, but I'm able to maintain my balance. Fuck, it's been a long time.

"I asked you," I say, trying to form my words. It's amazing how fast I get fucked up. Maybe I really *am* smoking too fast. Or maybe I'm just not used to this anymore. Maybe it's a combination of the two. "I asked you about the rope, dammit," I say, beating my fist on the table. Jason doesn't even flinch. He just grins, and he's so fucking sexy I want to grab him and throw him on the ground. But I hold back. I have to hold back. I have to let this unfold naturally. And even in my fucked up state, I know this.

"I've still got it," Jason says, putting the blunt back to his lips and taking a long inhale. "I've used it a lot."

"I've noticed."

And it's true. For years I've looked out the window and seen the men come and go from Jason's house. Each time, I was tempted to rush over there and beg him to take that rope and tie me with it. But I always refrained. Well… always, with one exception.

"You spying on me, kid?"

"Sometimes."

Now he laughs. "I figured that's why you liked having a bedroom window facing my house." He takes another hit before handing the blunt back to me. "Like fucking Gladys Kravitz."

"Who?"

"Nosy neighbor from a show you probably never heard of. Forget it."

I take another hit, and I do forget it. Now we're both high, and I wonder how I'm ever going to get past dad when I eventually go home.

"Put your feet up here, kid. Kick off your flip flops and just put them in my lap."

I don't question him. My cock jumps in my shorts and slowly slide my feet out of my flip flops, leaving them sitting right next to each other on the floor under the chair, and move my bare feet into his lap. For a moment, he studies them. He places his hands on them, and he moves his fingers between the toes.

"I remember that day," Jason starts to say.

"I've never forgotten it. Why didn't you do anything? You know I wanted it."

Jason moves his whole body forward, but he's wrapping his fingers around my ankles as he does so, just as I did last night when I woke up from my dream.

"You know I couldn't, Michael. You know that."

"Didn't stop me from wanting you to."

Now Jason sits back, throwing me some lewd stares, occasionally glancing back down at my feet. How soft they must look to him. Like soft, white bread. The bottoms of my feet have little bits of pink in them, and I notice Jason is observing my soles, as well. I furtively steal a glance at his crotch and notice the boner forming there. And I know well that he wants me. He wants me more than he's wanted any of those other men that have funneled in and out of his house over the years.

"No, it didn't. I'll admit that. But I never did anything. You know that."

"I know," I respond immediately. Jason wants reassurance. He's afraid of the law. Perpetually afraid. After all, he keeps pot on his kitchen table. He has guys coming over all the time. He had a horny teen in his house for a few years that wanted nothing more than to be tied and tickled without mercy and damn well nearly succeeded in convincing him to do just that. Plus, the pot makes Jason even more paranoid. He glances around as if it were at all possible someone were in the room with us, listening to our every word, waiting to slap some handcuffs on him and take him downtown.

"I'm 18 for Christ's sake," I say in a voice just a little too loud.

"Eighteen," Jason says, almost to himself. I almost laugh that Jason keeps saying that word, as if he's trying to decipher the meaning. Then he looks back at me, as best he can in his intoxicated state. "Yeah, you're 18. So what do you wanna do, kid?"

"You're the one that called out of work. What'd you have in mind?"

"I've got the rope back there." His eyes blaze with intensity. "I think you want this as bad as I do or worse."

"You have no idea."

Jason's cock is still hard as he places my bare feet on the floor and starts to stand and walk toward his bedroom. He turns, and his eyes burn with lust.

"You coming?"

"Yep."

I stand, holding onto the table so I don't fall over. My moment of ecstasy has finally arrived. A moment I've been awaiting for years.

CHAPTER 4

When I was 15, I had been smoking pot with Jason for a couple of years. What I didn't tell you, however, was that I frequently looked out my bedroom window to spy on him any time I could. Whenever he was going out the door for work, I tried to catch a glimpse of him as he hopped in his truck. There was something amazing about seeing him in his mechanic's uniform, how his arms bulged out of his short sleeves in the summer, how his tan face displayed such a serious look when he was on his way out the door.

One evening, I was looking out the window in exactly the same way, just as I did in the mornings. I don't know why, but I was. As I stared at Jason's house, I saw the door open, and I fully expected Jason to come out. Instead, another man I had never seen before walked out the door. It's not that I had never seen men come and go from Jason's house, but this one was different. He looked like he had seen a ghost.

"Hey. Come back," Jason said as he came out after the guy, shirtless and barefoot with a cigarette hanging out of his mouth. God he was sexy even then, even to me as a teenager. But this time, I knew something was wrong. I had always thought these men were just his buddies, just guys to come over and watch a ballgame or play a game of cards or smoke some pot as I did. It was on that evening that it dawned on me something far more exciting was at play. Jason was doing something sexual with these men, and as a budding teenager, I naturally wanted all the details.

It was innocent enough, and now was my opportunity. Why the guy leaving was so upset was beyond me, but I knew Jason would need some comforting, too. I was already wearing a tee shirt and some shorts, so I threw on some flip flops and made my way out the door. A moment later I was at his house, and I just walked in as I always did.

Jason was sitting at the kitchen table smoking a cigarette.

"How ya doing, kid?" He stared past me, as if in a daze. What was wrong with him?

"Who was that?" I asked.

"Some shithole that came over for a while. Don't worry about him."

My teenage inquisitiveness was getting the better of me, and I had no idea at the time that I was stepping into dangerous territory. So I moved forward full speed.

"What was he doing here? He looked pissed when he left."

Jason took another draw from his cigarette and let the smoke come out of his mouth, still looking past me. "He was pissed. Not what he expected."

"What did he expect?"

"Something normal, I guess."

I raised an eyebrow. "What'd you do to him?"

With those words, Jason leapt out of his seat and lunged for me. I was terrified as he grabbed me and pulled me further into the dining room, throwing me against the wall and looking straight into my eyes. I lost my flip flops in the process and stood there with wide eyes and bare feet as he pinned me there.

"Don't ask questions like that, kid," he said through gritted teeth. "You don't know what you're getting yourself into."

I was trembling, but there was some part of the whole experience that was hot. Having Jason manhandle me as he was doing was hot in and of itself, but having him be so rough with me was even hotter. And with my teenage hormones raging like they never really had before, I decided to move through my fear and push Jason even further.

"Let go of me, man."

Slowly, Jason let loose of my shirt, and I took a deep breath as he backed away. I could see his actions scared even him as he used his panic-stricken eyes to look into my own.

"I'm sorry, kid," he said. Then he sat back down and picked up his cigarette, puffing on it as he looked me over, his eyes making their way down to my bare feet.

I looked around the room, and on the sofa in the living room from where I stood, I saw it for the first time. A long piece of rope. It was strange seeing something like that in Jason's house.

"What's that?" I asked.

"Roll a blunt," Jason responded, nervously watching my curious eyes as I walked further toward the living room. "Roll a fucking blunt, kid. You don't wanna smoke?"

"Yeah, I want to," I said, but even as I spoke, I walked into the living room and took the rope in my hands, running my fingers over it.

"Get back in here."

"What's this for?"

"I said get your ass back in here, kid."

I stood for a moment longer and studied the rope. It was the soft nylon kind, and I can't explain the amazing electricity that surged through my body as I felt it in my fingers. I wondered what that rope would feel like wrapped around my wrists or my ankles. I looked down at my bare feet. I was too stupid at the time to put it all together, but I knew the rope was turning me on. I had jerked off since I was 11, but this would add a whole new element to the mix. It's as if I somehow discovered the fantasy of bondage on my own.

Suddenly, I felt Jason's strong hands on my shoulders and he whirled me around, grabbed the rope from my hands, and threw me on the couch. I was as terrified then as I was when he pinned me against the wall moments before.

"You're starting to piss me off," Jason said. God, he was so sexy when he was mad. It was hot. And some part of me, whether consciously or unconsciously, wanted to make him even angrier with me. I wanted him to be rough with me. But why? I couldn't figure it out. All I knew was it was hot as hell.

"What'd you do to that guy?" I asked.

Jason was still towering over me, and all I wanted was for him to jump on top of me, straddle me, and... I didn't know what. I just knew I wanted something. God, I just didn't know what it was. Jason stood there for a long time, the sexy anger flashing in his eyes as what I was starting to perceive as lust burned in them.

"Get out of here, kid. Come back sometime when you're not so nosy."

"I wanna know," I said.

"You're too young to understand, but I tied him up. He freaked out. Couldn't handle it."

"Why'd you tie him up?"

"Cause I wanted to!" Jason yelled, sitting down next to me. He picked up the remote and turned on the TV, probably hoping I'd stop asking these questions.

"Did he want you to?"

"He thought he did. But he didn't. A lot of times they don't know till they try it."

Jason stared straight ahead at the TV, not once looking at me. At least, not until I propped my bare feet up on the coffee table. To this day, I don't know why I did it. It just seemed so natural to relax at Jason's house.

"You've done it a lot?" I asked.

"Yep."

I don't know where the words came from, but come they did.

"You can tie me up," I said.

"Fuck, you really are stupid, aren't you? Giving you weed is one thing, but tying you up? They'd put me *under* the prison."

"Why?"

Jason rolled his eyes as he lit another cigarette. "Stupid kid. Go roll a blunt for Christ's sake. I'm not in the mood."

At that age, I was still unaware of the laws against sexual contact with minors, especially with any kind of BDSM play with them... and that's if I had even known what BDSM play was. All I knew was I really wanted Jason to tie me up. Again, I didn't know what I wanted him to do once he did so, but I wanted him to do it more than anything else. But how could I convince him?

"I want you to tie me."

"Ain't happening."

I tried to think. I had to think fast, too. Jason was getting more and more pissed, and I had to think of a way to convince him before he kicked me out for the day. And when he got mad, it was always a mystery how long he'd stay that way. Maybe a few days? A week?

"What about just my feet?" I asked. This was the oddest thing I could have thought of, as I didn't yet understand Jason's intense male foot fetish, but it made perfect sense to me. He could tie my feet for a few seconds, and I'd get to feel that rope around my bare ankles without Jason having to go further into this than he wanted. Besides, maybe he was just freaked out that the other guy was freaked out. He didn't know I trusted him unquestioningly, and he could do anything he wanted without any complaint from me.

I half expected Jason to stand up and get mildly violent with me again. Instead, he just looked over at me before grabbing the remote and turning off the TV.

"Hand me the rope," he said, "and put your feet in my lap. Just your ankles. Nothing else. And that's all. Nothing else." Jason pointed his finger at me, and his words were filled with a sense of seriousness I had never heard from him before. "Nothing. You got that."

"Yeah," I said, handing him the rope and putting my feet in his lap as he ordered. I was so engrossed in what he was doing, I was even afraid to blink. I didn't want to miss a second of this. The rope he held was probably four or five feet long. He doubled it over so he essentially had two strands of rope about two to two and a half feet long. Then he wrapped that rope around my ankles, running the loose strands through the area where the rope came together. It was ingenious how he tied me. I could tell he was an expert. He put his fingers between my ankles and the rope, most likely to ensure my circulation remained intact. Then he continued wrapping the rope around my bare ankles, and I curled my toes as my feet lay in his lap. Feeling that rope was the most exhilarating experience of my life.

When Jason was done, my bare feet lay in his lap with the rope wrapped around my ankles. It was hot! I can't describe it any other way. Jason stared lasciviously at my naked feet, and I continued curling my toes as I felt the glare of his eyes burning into my soft, young flesh. He grabbed the rope and picked my feet up off his lap, looking intently at my soles. I still didn't know what he found so fascinating, but he was giving me attention like he never had. He always called me kid, and this was the first time he wasn't actually treating me like one.

Then, suddenly, he ran his finger over my feet. I bent my knees and tried to pull away, but he grabbed the rope even tighter and pulled my feet back toward him.

"You said you wanted this, right kid?"

"Yeah." My voice was a breathy whisper as the remnants of that electrifying tickling still coursed through my body. It was the first time anyone had tickled me since my dad did when I was a kid.

Jason's breathing had grown heavy. I didn't know if he was pissed or if something else was bothering him. His fingers formed a claw, and it was as if he were fighting a battle in his own mind. His fingers moved further toward my young feet, and I gulped in anticipation of the tickling to come. I wanted it. More than anything.

Then, as disappointment would have it, he started untying me. He threw the rope on the ground and pushed my feet out of his lap.

"Get out," he said.

"What the..?"

"Get out!" This time he screamed, and his eyes were ablaze with fury, just as my own were filled with hurt. What had I done?

I stood and grabbed my flip flops, slipping them on and walking outside. Jason's throwing me out of his house was more terrifying even than his pinning me against the wall had been. Now I was even more confused. But I had also discovered my own new fetish, one that I intended to explore further, with or without Jason's help. And I knew just how to do it.

CHAPTER 5

I walk into Jason's bedroom, and he's right behind me, his hands on my shoulders. It's as if he's guiding me to his bed, and I see more rope lying there. I turn and face him. Our relationship – such as it is one – hasn't fully developed into one of romance. So I don't kiss him. Not yet. But I stare into his deep, blue eyes and notice the light stubble on his chin. God, he's so sexy. I can already imagine how hot it will be to feel his fingers running over my sides and pits and feet as he tortures me with insane tickling. I can hardly wait.

"You've wanted this for a while, huh?" he says.

I'm silent for a moment. Then I take a deep breath.

"Yeah," I say. I try to think of something to add to that, but I can't. It's the only word that gives justice to how I feel.

"Then get on the bed, and lie on your back," he says. He's breathing a little heavier now, and that breathing only intensifies as I pull off my shirt, leaving on my shorts, and get on the bed. My feet are already bare, so I soon find myself lying on the bed with my feet at the end and my arms stretched out at the head. Jason walks to his closet, and it's filled with rope. He must have it organized by length, and he pulls out four strands, maybe 8 feet long a piece. Then he walks to the head of the bed on my right. My eyes grow wide as I see him kneeling down. I lean over and watch as he moves the rope around the rail of the bed before bringing the two strands left from it up to where my wrist is. He ties a square knot right where he wants to restrain my wrist, and then he takes the two remaining strands of rope and wraps them around the edge of my hand.

He's careful. He doesn't do anything to impede my circulation. My breathing is intensifying, as well, as I feel that soft nylon rope wrapping itself around my wrist. He puts his finger in between the rope and my skin, ensuring the restraints won't chafe when both he and I know I'll inevitably start struggling from the unmerciful tickle torture he plans to subject me to. When he finishes, he stands back and studies his work, verifying he tied me just tight enough, but not too tight.

"Test that," he says.

My arm is out to the side of his massive bed, and I try to pull it toward me. It doesn't budge. I try to move it in any direction, and I can't. I look up at Jason with a little panic on my face, although my growing cock in my shorts betrays the fact that I like this. Jason leans toward me, and in a moment of gentleness, he brushes his hand on my cheek. I open my mouth to speak, but no words come forth. Then Jason leans forward and presses his lips lightly into mine. But just for a moment. When he pulls back, my eyes are wide. Electricity.

That's the only word I can think of to describe the sensation of Jason's hot lips on my own.

"I've wanted to do that for a long time," he says. Then he walks to the other side of the bed and starts to repeat the process with the rope, wrapping it around my other wrist, ensuring the rope doesn't impede my circulation, having me test my bondage. I'm lying there with my hands tied tightly, but my bare feet are free.

"Eighteen," he says to himself. "God, you're so young, kid."

Even as he speaks, though, he walks to the foot of the bed, kneeling down and wrapping the rope around the right side of the bedframe and bringing it up to where my bare foot lies, tying a square knot before starting to wrap the rope around my ankle. My cock dances in my shorts as I lie here feeling that rope wrapping around my foot. The roughness of that rope against my skin. The restriction it brings to my movement. The entire experience of being a helpless, vulnerable young man for Jason to torture beyond my mind if he so chooses. I wait in eager anticipation for the delicious torment to come.

Once Jason has my other foot tied down, he looks at me, stands over me and admires his work. Here I lie, completely immobile. Jason crawls onto the foot of the bed and kneels between my tied bare feet. Now he scoots forward, an almost demonic look of pleasure on his face, and climbs onto my torso, straddling me, preparing to do his devilish work on my skin. I'm well aware he knows how to wake my nerve endings with his fingers. He did so years ago when he had my bare feet tied in his lap, and he'll soon do so again.

I barely even blink as I watch him. Just as he did years ago, his fingers form claws, and he starts moving them toward my young armpits. I suck in the air and hold my breath, but my eyes never come away from his hands. My head twitches from side to side as he gets closer; I try to see both his hands as they prepare to torture my young flesh with unbearable ticklish agony. His hands stop just over my pits, and I let out the air stored in my lungs. Jason, with a wicked grin on his face, lightly scrapes my pits with his evil fingernails. It's wonderful, and it's terrible. It's both. I yelp just a little, and I feel a light layer of perspiration forming all over my body as Jason backs away for a moment. Clearly, he wants to be silly. But just for a moment. Then he'll get serious. Very serious.

"What?" he asks.

"You tickled me," I say with a grin.

"Did I?"

"Yeah,"

"Like this?"

"No, please!" This time I clench my eyes shut as I feel him dancing his fingers over my young armpits. Now I'm laughing uncontrollably, moving my sweaty head from side to side, surely wearing a stupid grin on my face as he tickles me without mercy. My respirations are picking up, as is my heartbeat, and my cock is growing harder in my shorts as Jason straddles me, donning his sexy mechanic shirt. I view the stubble on his face and the gleam in his deep, blue eyes as he moves his fingers over my pits and then down to my ribs. I close my eyes again, breathing even harder.

My bare ankles tug hard at their restraints as he continues tickling me, showing me no mercy. I can tell he wants to tickle me more than he wants anything else in the world. I'm breathing harder now, and I'm flexing my toes at the foot of the bed. Jason occasionally looks down at my naked feet before turning back and fixing his eyes with my own. I feel the tickling grow deeper as he moves his fingers even further into my pits. My eyes grow even wider as he presses his fingers in, the pressure torturing my flesh with tickling like I've never felt in my entire life.

Jason continues torturing my body, and I continue bucking wildly under his dancing fingers. Then he stops and grabs my face. I'm panting as I stare back into his beautiful eyes. I feel his rough, calloused fingers clutching my cheeks, and his face contains an odd mixture of malice and kindness.

"Am I hurting you?" Jason asks.

I shake my head as best I can with him holding my face. "No. Keep going."

"Are you sure?"

"Yes, please."

With those words, Jason scoots backwards on the bed, coming off of my torso, and looks down at my bare feet. Once again, I'm flexing my toes while he stares at them. I lift my head just a little from where it lies, and I watch. He moves toward my right foot, kneeling in front of it and studying it. Then he stands and walks over to the nightstand, opening up the drawer. I watch in horny excitement, wondering what he's going to do next. He grabs some lube from the drawer, as well as a fork. Then he comes back and kneels in front of my right foot, just as he did before.

"Ever been tickled by a fork?" Jason asks as he opens the lube and starts pouring a little into his hands, moving it through his fingers and lightly brushing it along the soles of my feet. I wince as I feel his cool fingers on my soles, slicking them up for even more torment.

"No," I respond, laying my head back and closing my eyes, enjoying this brief respite from the tickle agony but simultaneously looking forward to the tickle hell to come. I look down at Jason again and see him grinning as he moves that lube over my sole. I'm still flexing my toes, and he grabs them.

"Straighten out your foot, kid," he says. I try, but it's hard. My reflexes cause me to flex it again. Jason takes the edge of the fork and lightly slaps my foot. "I told you to straighten it."

"Okay," I reply, laying my head back again and trying to obey. A moment later, Jason has my foot completely slick with lube.

Suddenly, I feel it.

"Oh shit!" I scream as my entire body tenses. My bare ankles pull in futility against the expert bondage Jason has put me in. I look down at my bare foot and see he's running the prongs of the fork up and down my soles, scraping them without mercy, sending me into a state of tickle hell and tickle bliss like I've never before experienced in my life.

"I'm just getting started," he says as he continues scraping my soles. I'm breathing harder and deeper now.

"Please," I beg, gasping for breath. The tickling is too much, and yet I want so much more than he's giving me. I want him to show no mercy on my young, barely legal, naked feet. I want him to torture me beyond my mind and make me suffer the tickle anguish that will send us both beyond the brink of orgasmic bliss. I want the bondage to be tighter, more restrictive, more bizarre. I want him to scrape my soles till I'm screaming with laughter, and even then, I want him to refuse me any mercy, no matter how much I beg.

And he's doing just that. Soon, he moves to my other foot. He puts lube on that foot just as he did my right one. Then I feel the prongs of the fork scraping the soles of that foot. I look down and see the light tufts of hair on my toes as they flex under the constraints of the tickle torture. And I realize this is all I've ever wanted. I realize this experience – this moment – is the pinnacle of my existence. How can I ever desire anything other than what Jason, this man I have surely loved as long as I've known him, is giving me? How can I aspire to anything greater than screaming with laughter as Jason tortures my soles?

I thank God my dad has surely gone to work by now. I know he would have heard my screams and come to investigate. But Jason and I are safe. I'm here for him to tickle. I'm his willing tickle slave – for life, if he wants. He can do anything he wants to me, and I'll obey. I'll engage in the sexiest, most bizarre role playing games he can invent. I'll submit my bare feet to his whims any time he wants. I'll be there for him, give him my young feet to torture with ticklish agony any time he so desires.

And I realize I want so much more than he's giving me even now. I want him to tie me in even harder positions. I want him to *really* torture me. Of course, it's possible to tickle me too hard, I suppose, but I have complete trust that Jason knows where that line is. He'll never hurt me. Never.

Jason stops. He's panting, but I'm *really* panting. My eyes are closed as I wait for the torture to continue. Jason throws the fork on the floor and crawls onto the bed next to me, rubbing my crotch with his hand. I look into his eyes, and I realize he's sexier now than he's ever been – and he's *always* been sexy.

"I'm not done with you yet, kid," he says, once again brushing my cheek with his hand. I bite my lower lip in anticipation of what's to come next. I'm ready for so much more. More tickling. More bondage. More.

CHAPTER 6

The night after Jason tied my feet and lightly tickled them when I was 15, I instantly started obsessing over the experience. I had, in that one moment, discovered the joys of connecting on some sexual level with another man. I just didn't yet know what that meant. So that night after my dad went to bed, I sneaked into the computer room and got on the Internet. I had never looked for any kind of porn before or even had any interest in doing so. But I was still sophisticated enough to know how to delete an Internet history and ensure no one with normal knowledge of computers and web surfing could detect my activity.

I turned on the computer and pulled up Google. For several minutes, I simply sat and stared at the screen. What was I supposed to search for? Other than doing stupid homework assignments for school and somewhat obsessively checking my Facebook page, I had never done this. Why? I don't know. Other boys in school had talked about looking at pictures of naked women online, but I could never understand the appeal. In that moment, however, I was staring at a computer screen, wondering what in the name of God to even search for.

"Gay porn," I typed into the Google search bar, mouthing the words as I did so. A few images popped up along with millions of potential websites. *This should be entertaining*, I thought to myself as I scrolled through. Still, there was nothing on there of any interest. Black men fucking white men's mouths with 10 inch dicks did nothing for me, and I would eventually realize such porn did nothing for Jason either. How could I narrow this down? There was so much.

I didn't yet know about fetish porn and that everything in the world had a fan. I didn't know some men were into trannies or balloons or vampires or even jockstraps. Or feet. Or tickling. Jason's tying my feet together struck a chord with me, but I still didn't understand it. It was the first time I had even given the slightest thought to such activity, and yet it was the most powerful sexual experience of my life. Beating off every day or so had never led me to fantasies like that. I fantasized about boys at school, yes, but I have to confess I also fantasized about Jason with a cigarette hanging out of his mouth, wearing his mechanic's shirt and holding me down, forcing his lips onto my own. I suppose I was at least romantic enough for that, but I was soon to find out just how much of a taste for kink I really possessed.

"Feet," I typed in, again mouthing the word. Some Wikipedia article came up along with tons of sites about female feet. Gross! I immediately put the cursor back in the search bar and made a new search for "men's feet."

Now I was getting closer. A few pictures came up, and they were hot. I clicked on Google's Images tab, and all sorts of exciting pictures were displayed on the screen.

Wait.

There were even pictures of male feet tied together. I was getting still closer. My cock was growing hard in my shorts, and I reached down and started rubbing it. I had never felt heroin such as this coursing through my veins. Looking at these pics was even better than smoking weed. Hell, smoking weed would probably only enhance the experience. I was learning how to narrow my search, but Google wasn't working. What was that site the guys at school were talking about? Xtube? Yeah, that was it.

I typed in Xtube.com and clicked the button confirming I was 18 before clicking that I was a man interested in men. I have to admit I was slightly nervous the site's owners might have some way of finding out my real age. But still I pressed on. I was so close. Nothing would stop me.

"Male feet tickled," I typed into the search bar on Xtube. Fuck! There were so many videos of men getting tickled by other men. Some of them were even tied. I scrolled through, checking out each one. There were pages and pages of them. I could spend the rest of the month just looking at these videos.

And there had to be more. Many more. There were other sites. Other fetishes. I knew then I had discovered a whole new way to spend my time. A new universe waited to be explored! And yet, something was different.

I had taken my first hit of the heroin that *is* Internet porn. I would never be the same.

I set the volume as low as I could to avoid disturbing my father, and I looked through as many of those videos as I felt I had time to before I would shoot my load without even having the opportunity to watch one of them. After searching for a few minutes through what seemed like a million thumbnails leading to videos, I finally selected one. The thumbnail looked interesting enough. The tickler had a rugged appearance and a mean look on his face; in fact, he reminded me much of Jason. He had that sexy, blue collar appearance I found so appealing in my next door neighbor. I clicked on the thumbnail and licked my lips in anticipation of the tickling scene to come. There was something so electrifying about having Jason tie my bare feet together on his lap and lightly tickle my soles. But this would be even *more* electrifying.

Why had I selected this video? Was it because the tickler was hot like Jason? Or was it because the ticklee was hot? No. Neither. It was because the video displayed an older tickler – a man in his late 20's – tormenting a guy in bondage that couldn't have been 18 very long. The video's thumbnail reminded me so much of my own fantasy, I could feel my heart pounding in my chest as I got ready to watch.

The ticklee was sitting in a pair of stocks. He was shirtless and barefoot with his bound feet sticking out in front of him. They were probably size 8 or 9, and he clearly wasn't a very big guy. The tickler was standing nearby, asking all kinds of questions.

"What's your name?"

"John."

"How old are you, John?"

"Eighteen."

This would be perfect. The tickle torture hadn't even started, but just the bondage and the sweet exchange between tickler and ticklee was enough to make me reach down and start stroking my already rock hard dick in my shorts. I kicked my flip flops off underneath me, wanting to feel my bare feet against the carpet, wanting to feel as vulnerable as that young man in the video surely did. I watched the model's face. It was filled with wonder, excitement, fear. I wanted to feel all those things myself as Jason had *me* tied in the strictest bondage – something like the stocks that model was bound in. And I wanted him to take all kinds of cruel tickling tools to my feet and upper body and make me squirm in his arms. I wanted him to gain pleasure from my torture. I wanted him to want me. More than anything.

The tickler started by lightly running his fingers over John's small bare feet. Instantly, John started flexing his toes, and his body shifted nervously from side to side. The sweat already started forming on his young body as the tickler grew even more intense with the torture he was inflicting on the boy. As I watched, stroking my cock, I imagined that *I* was that model, that *Jason* was tickling me, starting light but knowing how strong I was and how I would go to the end of the earth to please him. Even if it meant taking the most insane, unbearable tickle torture he could dish. What was it about those few seconds that afternoon that had captivated me to the point of wanting to be tied in restrictive, humiliating bondage and make myself completely vulnerable to Jason? Did I trust him that much?

The answer was yes.

Did I love him?

Well, did I *love* him?

I wasn't sure. I just knew I trusted him, and I knew I could grow to love him in time. Who knows? Maybe with more tickle play, I could come to love him even sooner.

The tickler's fingers moved even faster over the boy's soles. He crinkled his face and the flesh on his feet as he laughed. The sweat glistened on his forehead, and his perfect teeth gritted in his mouth as he violently pulled against the tight restraints that bound him. Bang! Bang! As he violently tugged against the foot bondage, the stocks made that kind of knocking noise, but the tickler was relentless. He tickled the boy without mercy, soon moving to his upper body.

The model's eyes grew wide as he watched the tickler move closer to his pits, holding his fingers there for a moment to increase the boy's terror.

"No!" he screamed, closing his eyes and violently shaking his head, tiny beads of sweat flying from his cheeks as he prepared for the imminent torture to come.

Then it happened.

The tickler dug into the boy's pits without mercy. The screaming was exhilarating as I watched, as I fantasized I was that boy getting my own pits worked over and that Jason was the sadistic master working them over. I was dripping precum in my shorts as I watched the spectacle. The boy in the video was now pulling against the restraints that held his arms out to the side, secured with several straps going up and down his arms. They wouldn't budge. They were silent, impartial witnesses to the boy's torture as they held him in place and forced him to fully experience every second of the tickling on his pits.

And the tickler wasn't just dancing his fingers over the boy's pits. Oh, he was certainly doing that, too. But he was also *digging* his fingers into the model's flesh, forcing the boy to release tortured laughter deep from his gut as he leaned forward as far as he could, a futile effort to escape the insane tickle torment.

A moment later, the tickler stopped, and the boy sat in his restraints, panting, nervously watching as the tickler moved back to his feet.

"Are we done?" the boy asked, his eyes filled with innocence and daring to show just a little hope for mercy. But the tickler was silent, and he was out of the line of the camera for a moment, clearly searching for something. When he came back to the boy's feet, the boy screamed once again.

"No! You can't! Please, it's been ten minutes already! Please!"

Then the tickler showed the boy a hairbrush he held in his hand, something I would soon find out from my newfound love of porn was a ticklee's worst nightmare, and he made sure the boy had a chance to get a good look at it. The boy slowly shook his head this time, only mouthing the word "no."

I would one day find out myself just how hellish the tickle torture from a hairbrush can be. Even then, before I knew I would experience such delicious agony, I stroked my cock to the fantasy.

The tickler held the hairbrush a few inches from the boy's feet, stiff and cruel bristles facing his soles. Then the ticker started running the bristles of that hairbrush over the boy's young feet, and this time the model's reactions were so powerful, I thought he might actually break his restraints. But he didn't. Those restraints remained the silent witnesses to this torture they had been since it started, and the boy's sweat only increased on his body as the tickling ensued like mad for at least four or five more minutes.

How much more could this boy stand? Did he need water? Was he hungry? Did the tickler and the boy know each other before, as Jason and I did? Were they friends? Was this just about the money? All these questions ran through my head as I stroked my cock, getting closer and closer to shooting my load, hoping beyond all hope that dad was upstairs asleep and not hearing the tickle torture happening on his computer screen just a few feet beneath him.

A moment later, I shot my hot load all over my chest, and I lay against the chair panting. Instantly, I stopped the video and returned to Google. Then I deleted the Internet history as best I knew how before wiping up the cum with my underwear and slipping my flip flops back on. I had to make it back upstairs without my dad hearing. That probably wouldn't be too hard. Yes, he had good ears, but even if he caught me, I could always just come up with some lie on the spot. He'd never suspect I'd do something like this.

Pot had been my drug for a few years. Now I had found a new one. Gay Internet fetish porn. It was all I would ever need. But even that drug paled in comparison to my fantasies with Jason. After I went to bed a few minutes later – and even after having cum harder than I ever had in my entire life – I started stroking my cock again, this time fantasizing that I was that boy in the stocks and that Jason was the tickler. In my fantasy, he was standing in front of my young, bare feet preparing to tickle the shit out of me.

I came again, and again I lay there panting. This was a new adventure. One I would never let go of. I just had to find a way to convince Jason to tickle me for real. Little did I know at the time it would be a few years before I would be able to appreciate that luxury.

CHAPTER 7

Slowly, even as I drink in every moment of my bondage, Jason unties me. First my bare feet, then my wrists are free. I reach for my right wrist with my left hand and rub the circulation back in. Jason didn't tie me too tightly, but it's still good to have a break.

He's staring at me, but it takes me a minute to notice. As I'm rubbing my wrists and then move down to rub my ankles, I finally see his eyes, and my own lock with his. What is he thinking as he stares at me with a countenance of lust, love, confusion, playfulness, and even malice? It's like he enjoys torturing me, and yet he wants me to enjoy the experience, as well.

"Ready for more, kid?" he asks with a mischievous grin on his face. Fuck! Does he want more already? He just untied me, and now he wants to do this again. And the answer is yes. I want more bondage, more tickling, more restriction. I want the bondage to be more bizarre, harder core, more difficult. I want him to leave me breathless with bondage and tickle torture. I want him to give me more than I can stand. Well, maybe not *too* much, but still more than I can stand. And I want to take it for my tickle master like a good tickle slaveboy should.

"Yes Sir," I say, and then I sit back and blink. It doesn't occur to me why I called him sir. Maybe it's from watching a few porn videos years ago in which the sub called the dom sir. Maybe it's just the natural instinct of a tickle slaveboy like me. But whatever caused me to address him with this title of immense respect, he grins at me, sitting down next to me and grabbing a cigarette and a lighter off the nightstand.

"I like it when you call me sir," he says. "You're a good kid."

I don't respond. What can I say to that? I want to be a good kid. A good kid for my tickle master. A good kid in bondage as my master runs his fingers without mercy over my young armpits and boyish looking feet. I take a deep breath, smelling the fresh smoke pouring off the end of his cigarette as he stares at me with a grin, occasionally putting the cigarette back to his lips and taking a puff.

"You're flexible," he says, though his intonation leaves me wondering if he's making a statement or asking a question.

"Yeah," I respond, probably leaving him confused as to whether I'm acknowledging that statement or asking my own question. But it's not enough. I'm horny, and I want to move this forward. "I can take it. A lot of it."

"Tickling?"

"That, yeah. And bondage. I can take a lot more."

Jason grins again as he puts his cigarette butt out in a nearby ashtray before lighting another one. I look down at his crotch, and his cock is growing harder and harder. He wants this. He wants it bad. Finally, he finishes his next cigarette. And I'm dying from the anticipation.

"Come in the other room," he says, grabbing a few pieces of rope and a pillow as he stands to walk back into the dining room. Fuck! What does he have in mind now?

I get up and follow him, clad only in my shorts, my bare feet padding against the floor as I walk. The carpet of the bedroom under my bare feet soon turns into the hard tile of the kitchen as we walk toward the table. Jason pulls out a chair, and then he stares at me again with a lascivious grin on his face.

The chair looks simple enough. It's just a normal seat with an opening in the back like you often see around a cheap dining room set.

"Flexible huh?" he says.

"Yes Sir."

"Good," he responds with a nod. He puts the pillow on the seat of the chair in front of him. "Get on the chair on your knees and put your feet through the back."

I look at that chair for a moment longer, and then I slowly obey. It's awkward at first, but I soon kneel onto the pillow on the chair, which is facing the table. Then I put my feet behind me, resting them against the edge of the pillow hanging out of the opening as I sit down on my knees and wait for my tickle master to continue. Surely he's not going to tie me to this chair. How would he do that?

I look over and see the rope he's holding, and he gets behind me. Lightly, he tickles the soles of my bare feet sitting right next to each other as they rest at the edge of the back of the chair. I giggle and move around a little, a weak protest to the tickling. My bare soles crisscross, each one in turn trying in futility to protect the other. Then Jason stops, and once again I feel the electrifying sensation of that nylon rope as he wraps it around my bare ankles. I suck in the air and hold my breath for a moment, waiting for him to finish my ankle bondage. I'm in no position to ask questions. A slaveboy like me never is. I realize this as my confused emotions get further and further wrapped up in the man Jason is and was and has become.

"Move your hands over your shoulders, kid," he orders, and I instantly obey, wondering how much more salty sweat will form on my brow when he inevitably starts putting me through the rigors of tickle torture again. But I can take it. I can take anything for Jason. I'm forming a bond with him that I may never be able to break. And I pray to whatever gods will listen that he's forming the same bond with me.

Jason moves some rope around my wrists, again placing his finger between the rope and my skin to ensure no chafing occurs, and then he takes the slack of that rope and brings it down to my feet, securing it there. I look around, nervously moving my head from side to side as I realize my predicament. I'm tied in a precarious situation. I could fall over and bring the chair with me, and that wouldn't be a pretty accident at all. I turn and look at Jason with panic-stricken eyes, and then I realize he hasn't let go of me. He's still holding me, still taking care of me as his tickle boy.

"I'm not gonna let you fall over," he says, still holding me while grabbing another piece of rope. Then he takes that rope and starts wrapping it around my torso and securing me more safely in the chair. He even takes the slack of that rope and ties it to the front legs of the table to keep the chair from falling over. He's thought of everything. How much I'll buck around when he tickles the shit out of me again. How to keep me from falling over when that inevitably happens.

He walks to the pantry, and I turn my head, watching his every move. Then he comes back with some oil.

"I forgot the lube in there," he tells me, "and it looks like your soles could use another coat."

"Yes Sir."

Jason kneels behind me and put some of that vegetable oil into his hands, running it over my soles and getting them nice and slick again for the torture to come. As he rubs the oil in, he lightly tickles my bare feet behind me. I try to lift my body up, but then I realize my hands are tied securely to my bare feet behind me. Even in something as innocuous as a chair tie, Jason has thought of everything. I'm completely immobile. Again.

"Please," I say. It's more an exhale than a word. I close my eyes, my toes twitching in their bondage behind me, and I wonder what Jason has in store for me next. His hands leave my feet. Now I open my eyes again, and Jason is nowhere to be seen. Fuck! How did he get out of here so fast? Where did he go?

I don't call out. It seems pointless, and I trust Jason without question. I know he'll *never* hurt me. I know he'll take good care of his tickle slaveboy and make me enjoy this experience at least as much as he does, if not more. A moment later, I turn my head again and see Jason coming out of the bathroom holding a hairbrush. It's a long brush with stiff bristles. And I'm not some stupid 15-year-old kid anymore. Now I'm a man, and I know well what he plans to do with that brush. The bristles are stiff enough that they'll rack the most horrendous tickle torture on my young, soft, bare feet. And they're hard enough that it will cause only the slightest pain, but I also know that the very light pain will be sexy and that it will only add to the tickle agony Jason plans to put me through.

Still, I continue my panic. But only a little. I pull at my restraints. I try to cross my bare feet behind me at the ankles, but I can't. Fuck! Jason stands and watches me struggle with an amused look on his face.

"Think you can get away, kid?" he asks, toying with me. Then he walks to my chair and puts his hand on my shoulder. The simple exchange of energy in that sexy touch is enough to calm me instantly. I stop struggling. I'm ready to take whatever torture Jason wants to inflict on my young, bare feet and even my upper body.

For a moment, I stare forward, waiting to find out what Jason will do. Will he attack my bare feet as he was doing earlier? Will he dig into my young pits? Will he reach around and start running his fingers over my abs, causing me to lean forward and laugh to the point of ticklish tears? I'm soon to find out.

Then, without warning, Jason starting running his fingers over my ribs.

"Fuck!" I shout. I wasn't expecting this because I had been too busy staring forward, daydreaming. Now Jason is moving his fingers over my ribs, and I'm dancing in my chair as much as my cruel restraints will allow. But now he's doing something I didn't anticipate. The pressure is increasing. He's pressing his fingers just a little harder into my ribs. And then a little harder still. Fuck!

I start fighting with my restraints. The tickling is heaven and hell at the same time. I wonder how much more I can stand, and yet I'm determined to take as much as Jason wants to give me. I'm determined to be the perfect tickle slave that that stupid guy who left his house pissed off years ago just couldn't be for him. I'm determined to make it so Jason will never want to tickle anyone but me ever again.

I'm determined to make him love me. Can I do that?

Can I make him love me?

I continue moving around uncontrollably, grateful Jason placed a pillow in the chair. My toes are spasmodically flexing behind me even though my young, bare feet are not currently the object of his attack. But that changes soon enough.

Finally, Jason gives my ribs a moment of rest, and I'm panting. Once again, my body is completely covered in sweat, and even though I can't see him, I can *feel* him kneeling behind me. He brushes my feet with his fingers, but just once. I jump a little at the surge of energy that moves through my whole body with that one touch. Then Jason grabs my bare feet by the ankles and holds them in place, just as the rope is doing. What's he going to do? Fuck!

Then I remember it.

The hairbrush.

I start shaking my head violently and pulling against the rope restraining my bare ankles.

"No," I say. "Please, no."

"What are you gonna do, kid?"

"Please Jason." I turn to him, and my big eyes meet his. For a moment he stops, but I look at his hand, and his fingers are still tightly clutching the hairbrush. He takes his other hand and brushes my cheek, just as he's done several times already today.

"You can handle this, kid," he says. Then he leans forward and plants a light kiss on my lips. I swoon. I *can* handle this. Anything for Jason. Anything.

He kneels behind me again and places the bristles of the hairbrush against my bare soles so they run all the way across the heels of both my feet. I close my eyes and hold my breath. I must look like I'm praying, but I'm not. I'm scared. And not just of the imminent tickle torture, although I'm scared of that, too. I'm scared of disappointing the man I have loved since I was remotely old enough to feel such a strong emotion, even if I didn't understand what it was at the time.

Jason doesn't give me a chance to warm up. He starts moving that hairbrush over my soles, scraping my bare feet up and down, up and down. I throw my head back, and the sweat is now running into my eyes.

"Fuck! Oh please, Jason! Fucking Jesus Christ!" I cry out, but Jason is unmerciful in his torture. His means of communication with me in that moment *is* torture. And he knows I can take it. That's why he's torturing me as bad as he is. He knows – and maybe has always known – that deep within this young man who was only days before a kid is now a tickle slave waiting to be sorely abused with the most insane tickle torture a man could ever imagine.

Those bristles are now torturing my feet without mercy. I'm still pulling against my restraints, still begging Jason for a moment of respite I ironically pray not to receive. Regardless, he's not giving me any. He's relentless in his torture, scraping my soles with that hairbrush. My boyish looking feet are starting to ach as my feet and toes flex under the merciless constraints of the tickle torture.

"Hold still, Michael," Jason says. When he says my name, I swoon again. He almost always calls me "kid," but to hear him speak my name only makes my cock jump in my shorts. Now I'm trembling. I'm trying to hold still, and for a moment I succeed. Jason is still moving the hairbrush over my soles, but he's also watching my face. I know he likes the appearance of concentration in my boyish looking eyes, a look of intense attempt to obey him, to hold still. And he likes the appearance of a boy's face he knows will break at any moment.

And break I do. Once again, I throw my head back, this time pulling with my arms as Jason continues torturing my bare soles. He has his fingers wrapped around my ankles to even further restrict their movement, and he's moving the hairbrush up and down, back and forth. He's making figure 8's with it. It's like a punishment. A punishment my dad never gave me. And in my fantasy, I'm taken back to my childhood. Jason is like my older brother picking on me, asserting his authority while simultaneously demonstrating his love. He's picking on me only to the extent I can take it, but no more. But he also knows I'm a good slaveboy, and that means I can take a lot. I can take even more than the torture he's currently giving me. And I'm soon to find out just how much more.

Jason takes the hand on my ankles and moves it, wrapping his fingers around my big toes. He holds my big toes in place and doesn't let go. No matter how much I try to fight him, I can't escape. I can't use one foot to crisscross with the other and offer the other foot even a moment of respite. Now he can tickle both my feet at the same time, and neither foot can receive even a second of mercy. Now I know what it is to be fully present, fully in the moment. Now I have to experience every agonizingly slow second of torture as Jason moves the brush over my bare feet.

The sweat must surely be covering my whole body now, causing me to glisten in the light of the room. My screams go unheard or ignored by the neighbors, many of whom are elderly and can't hear very well anyway. And still, Jason presses on, running the hairbrush over my soles. Now I long for anything to stop the torture. Jason really is taking it too far. But I have faith in him as the perfect tickle master. Even now, I know he won't cross the line. I can take it. Anything for Jason.

And just as suddenly as the torture started, it stops, and I lean forward as much as my bondage will allow, panting in my chair tie. I lift my head to look up at Jason, and I realize I don't know how much time has passed since he stopped tickling me? Has it been a minute? Ten minutes? All I know is Jason is standing in front of me with a cup of ice water.

"Here," he says, putting the cup to my mouth. I greedily drink my fill, and he even goes back to the sink to get some more. He brings me a second cup, and I shake my head, trying to refuse.

"No," I say. "I've had enough."

"You need to stay hydrated, kid," Jason says, and an order from my tickle master is all I need to try to take just a little more water. "Besides, I have more in store for you. Are you already spent, or can you take any more?"

I'm growing dizzy. I had thought Jason couldn't take the tickle torture too far, but now the slightest doubt is etching itself into my brain. *Can* he take it too far?

"I'll do anything you want, man," I say, looking him in the eye. His eyes are soft, but they have a mischievous glare in them. I know he's not finished torturing me. After all, he's still fully dressed and hasn't even begun to get off. How much longer does he plan to tickle me? An hour? All day? I don't know. I only know I'll do my best to take whatever torture he plans to inflict upon me. I'm his tickle slave. For life if he wants. And if he wants to love me, I'll take that, too. No questions asked.

CHAPTER 8

Every night for a week I had sneaked into the computer room to search for more tickling videos. Jason had grown more distant during that time, but he was already starting to come back around. Still, the drug of gay Internet fetish porn was continuing to course through my veins as I turned on the screen and got ready for another Xtube visit. Even the hum of the machine and the light of the computer glowing in the dark room was starting to affect the strong feelings of sex in my groin. At 15, I was already hooked. And I was getting away with it. Dad was oblivious to my activity – somehow. What I didn't realize in that precise moment, though, was that the events that occurred over the next hour would change the course of my life for several years to come.

By that point, I had begun to perfect my Xtube search terms and experiment with new ones. I had even discovered the real fetish porn sites such as barefootbound.info, which focused on naked male tickling and bondage, but I didn't have access to a credit card to subscribe. So I had to satisfy my nightly urges with Xtube.

I put in a new search term, finding that often the same videos were coming up no matter what I entered. But it didn't matter. The videos seemed endless, and people were creating new ones all the time.

"Male feet tickled in bondage," I put into the search box, again mouthing the words as I typed. I almost salivated as I waited a few seconds for the video thumbnails to show up. And although I wasn't conscious of it at the time, I at least subconsciously knew what my taste was. Older tickler. Younger ticklee. Heavy bondage. Yeah, that's what I liked.

I started scrolling through the videos, and I found that the further I got into my porn usage, the longer it took me to find anything I really liked. It seemed the selection process contained its own pleasures I was only starting to become familiar with. Finally, I found a video I thought would do the job. This one, again, was a younger man of about 19-years-old tied in a hogtie. He was on a bed in a nice room, and once I started playing the video, he immediately began pulling against his restraints. He wasn't just tied with rope though. No, this was professional bondage. Someone had put wrist and ankle cuffs on that guy with an O-ring on each one to move the rope through. After about a minute of struggling, the boy was starting to get sweaty, and I was already stroking my cock as I watched. The look in his eyes was both desperate and defiant at the same time, possibly something the video's producer told the boy he was looking for.

Then, a moment later, the tickler came in. He was a taller man dressed in normal clothes. He, too, was barefoot, but he wore a tank top and shorts. He was also older – even older than Jason. He was probably in his 30's, as he had brown hair with just the slightest touches of gray. And his eyes were a deep green. He wore a wicked look on his face as he watched the boy struggle, preparing to tickle torture him beyond the brink of insanity.

The tickler crawled onto the bed and grabbed the boy's hogtied bare feet. The boy closed his eyes and held his breath as the tickler prepared to run his finger's over that boy's soles. Like Jason, the tickler formed a claw with his fingers and moved them to the boy's foot flesh, holding them in place for a moment to add to the boy's terror before beginning the real torture. The boy kept his eyes closed, and there was something about the fact that each of them had just the lightest layer of fresh sweat covering their bodies that added to the eroticism of that particular video.

Again, I kept the volume low to avoid disturbing my father, but I could barely hear it myself. I wanted to *really* hear this boy's screams for mercy as the tickler ravaged his bare soles. So I turned up the volume – but just a little – and watched as the tickle torture began. The boy clenched his eyes shut even tighter and started bucking around on the bed. His laughter wasn't exactly high pitched, but it wasn't a low, gruff laughter either. It was cute as hell, though. I loved the way he gritted his teeth, and I loved seeing the tickler's delighted facial expressions as he mercilessly moved his fingers over the boy's soles.

A moment later, the sexy older tickler grabbed a hairbrush – seemingly common in tickle videos. At the time, I didn't know if the hairbrush really was harder for a ticklee to bear or if the videos' producers simply told the models to start bucking a little more wildly when the tickler brought out that instrument of tickle torture, but regardless, that's exactly what happened.

"No! I can't! I can't!" he screamed as the tickler cruelly moved the hairbrush over the boy's hogtied bare feet. The boy flexed his toes in his bondage, but I wanted to hear his laughter. I wanted the fullest experience of the torture I could have, even if it was far short of experiencing that torture firsthand. I turned the volume up just a little more, just enough to hear him pleading for mercy.

A moment later, the door behind me clicked, and instantly the light flipped on in the computer room. I immediately moved into action and paused the video before turning off the screen. But I didn't act fast enough. Fuck! Why hadn't I just closed the Internet browser?

"What are you doing?" my dad asked, his sleepy eyes viewing me.

I was silent. And I was caught. What could I say? He was wearing his bathrobe, and I was shirtless and barefoot, wearing only a pair of shorts to cover my growing teenage erection. He came closer to me, but I knew he wouldn't be violent. Still, that didn't stop me from being terrified. Terrified of the shame he was about to put me through. Dad was a psychologist, after all, so he knew well how to make his son feel shame.

He towered over me, breathing slowly, clearly trying to avoid losing his temper. He cocked his head to the side, and I could see him trying to hide the intense anger on his face. He knew what I was doing. How could he not?

"Turn on the screen."

"Dad..."

"Turn it on." He was still as calm as he could possibly be under these circumstances. But even being afraid of him, I didn't move. Even being afraid of what he would do to me or how he might punish me, I was still more afraid of his discovering my secret fetish. It's not that I had a problem with him knowing I was gay; I knew he'd accept that without question. But for Dad to know beyond a shadow of a doubt that I was into bondage and tickling would be too much even for him.

I sat still as a statue, my eyes twitching as I looked up at him. Slowly, he leaned forward and turned on the screen.

What had been a great delight for me only moments before suddenly became a source of horror as my dad stood and stared at the still shot of that video on the monitor. For several moments he was silent, and I didn't dare look him in the eye. I couldn't look at the video either. I simply stared off in another direction, feeling the heat burning on my face at having been caught in the darkest secret of my life.

"Play the video, Michael," he said, his voice just cool enough to be chilling.

Again, I hesitated, but without waiting another moment, Dad reached over me and put his hand on the mouse, moving the cursor to the video and continuing where it had left off.

"Please!" the boy screamed as the merciless tickler grabbed his hogtied bare feet even tighter and moved his fingers over his soles. The boy's toes scrunched, and his the wrinkles on his soft, young flesh testified to the merciless torture his tormentor was inflicting on him. He closed his eyes and screamed, laughed, begged. But the tickler was relentless.

My hardon was gone, though. All I could think of was the humiliation that came with my dad having caught me looking at my favorite type of porn – a type of porn that, even as a psychologist, he could never come to accept in his own son.

I finally mustered the courage to look up at my dad, but he was simply staring at the screen, a clear look of disapproval on his face. Then he looked down at me.

"Turn it off," he said. Immediately, my hand went to the mouse. I not only stopped the video, but I also closed the whole browser, cursing the fact that I couldn't delete the Internet history again. Of course it didn't matter now that Dad knew my dirty little secret. Dammit, why couldn't I simply have left the volume as low as I had on other nights?

Dad walked away from me and ran his fingers through his hair. Then he turned back to me, his eyes ablaze.

"What the hell are you doing, Michael?"

I was trembling. Was it the shame? Fear of punishment? I don't know. But I trembled before my father all the same.

"Answer me!" he said, raising his voice. Still I was silent. "Do you know," he continued, "that I have all kinds of patients? I see CEO's with millions of dollars in their personal checking accounts, and I see people getting ready to get kicked out on the street. But if they tell me they look at porn all the time, that's the one thing they have in common that ruins them." Dad was now standing over me, and all I could do was look up into his fiery eyes. "Porn ruins men's lives, Michael. It absolutely ruins their lives. I've seen marriages destroyed and jobs lost. I've seen men go to prison, for God's sake! And all because they got into the very thing I just caught you doing."

"Dad..." I tried to stand up, but my old man pushed me back into the chair. My fear took me over again, and I didn't dare move.

"It was Jason who taught you this, wasn't it?"

"No," I said, the panic surely clear in my eyes.

"That man got you into this. I know he did. I don't know what you do when you go over there, but I knew something was going on."

"Dad, there's nothing going..."

Dad pointed his finger at me, and my words stopped halfway out of my mouth. The silence was deafening. It was like waiting for an atomic bomb that was inevitably going to explode any moment but simply hadn't yet.

"Give me your cell phone," he said through gritted teeth.

"What?"

"You're grounded. Until further notice." He waited a moment. Then he shouted, "Give it to me!" Trembling, I grabbed it off the computer table and reluctantly handed it to him. My cell phone was my connection to the world. In grounding me, it felt as if he were trying to disconnect me with humanity.

"I'm putting some software on your phone that will report your Internet activity to me."

"But that's not fair!"

"And you are *never* to use this computer again unless I'm sitting in here with you. Do you understand?"

"Dad!"

"I'm putting a password on it. If you need to use it, you can do it with me watching." I was breathing uncontrollably, praying as hard as I could Dad would never say the next words that came from his lips. "And you can never see Jason again."

"What? Not ever? No! You can't do this!"

"Not for the balance of your natural life!" I had never seen fury in Dad's eyes like I saw as he stood before me, demonstrating he had the power at least to make me believe he was wrecking my life.

I remember when the first tear started flowing down my cheek. It wasn't when my dad walked into the room or when he tried to shame me while making me play the video in front of him. No, it was when he told me I could never see Jason again. And at that time, it didn't occur to me that I could still see him when I was old enough not to have to obey orders from my dad. After all, 18 seems a long way off when you're 15.

"Please!" I said, the tears flowing freely from my eyes. It was in that moment that I realized – even if only subconsciously – that I loved Jason. More than anything.

"Go to bed, Michael," my dad said in a bitter voice, walking out with my phone clutched in his hand and flipping the light switch on his way out, leaving me in darkness. And darkness was all I could understand in that moment. Darkness had suddenly become more familiar to me even than my own father.

CHAPTER 9

The next day was Sunday, and I knew Jason didn't work on Sundays, so he'd surely be home. I didn't know if Dad had said anything to him that morning, as I was so distraught from the previous night's events, and it was entirely possible he had already gone to talk to him. But I knew I had to try to get to my next door neighbor before it was too late, before he fell out of my life for years. That's not something I felt I could bear.

The day was warm, so I threw on a tee shirt, a pair of shorts, and some flip flops. Then I sneaked out of the house and made my way over. Only this time, I knocked on the door. I never did that; I always just walked in. But that day after such a bizarre turn of events, it felt almost as if I were invading his privacy. I'd walk in if I had to, but I wanted to at least give Jason the chance to come to the door. When it finally occurred to me Jason wasn't coming, I looked in the window of his garage and saw his car, so I knew he was there. Fuck, why wasn't he answering? Then I went back to the door, turned the knob, and walked in.

"Hey," I called out. Saying his name seemed superfluous. He always called me "kid," and I often just called him "man" or nothing at all. But as I looked through his house, I finally tried using his name. "Jason!" I shouted, looking in the living room before finally making my way to his bedroom.

Suddenly, Jason came out of the bathroom. I jumped and stood back. It was like a bad horror flick except I knew deep down Jason would never hurt me. Not badly anyway. He grabbed me by the shoulders and pinned me against the wall, just as he had done before the day I got nosy about the rope and the man who had been at his house.

"What are you doing here?" he asked through gritted teeth.

"I had to see you."

"Your dad was over here this morning, kid. Do you know he threatened to call the cops?"

"Let me go!"

Jason slammed me against the wall. "He threatened to beat the shit out of me. Isn't your old man a shrink? Do they even do that?"

"Nah, he won't do that," I said, looking straight into his eyes with fear. "You could kick his ass anyway." A moment later he let me go, turning around, not daring to look me in the eye. Then he must have found new courage, and he turned back to face me.

"You can't come here anymore, Michael. It's too dangerous. You don't have anything to lose, but my whole life is at stake. Do you know what they'd do to me if anyone even *said* I was doing some shit with you?"

"Nobody's gonna think that, man. I never said that. Nothing."

Jason laughed bitterly. "That's not the point. If people think I'm messing around with a minor in *any* way, they'll could call the cops. Even if they don't, I could lose my job. My friends could think I'm some kind of sick pervert. And I'm not." Jason's voice was rising to a fever pitch. I had never seen him cry, but his eyes were growing moist. What was so upsetting to him? What was the big deal? Even then, I couldn't understand how all this would make him cry. "Maybe I *am* a pervert, Michael, but I'm not like that. I'm not gonna do anything that's gonna hurt either of us. You're looking at getting in trouble at home. You may get grounded or get your Internet activity monitored. But me?" he said, pointing to himself as he stepped back, clearly putting a cool distance between us. "I could get fucked in prison. I could get put on the Sex Offender Registry. My life could be over. And all because you looked at some shit on your computer that I didn't even tell you about. And your dad thinks I did. He thinks I'm doing stuff with you I'm not. And he thinks I'm some sort of twisted fucker that's molesting a minor." Jason's tears were flowing freely now. I had never seen him come apart like this. He put his hands in his face before pulling them away and looking back at me. "Like I said, I don't know what I feel. Maybe I *am* a sick man. But I'll be fucked if I go to jail over something like this.

"You're not going to jail, man."

"Get out."

"Jason, you don't understand."

Jason approached me again, standing in front of me with his nose just inches from my own. "If I don't go to jail for tying you up, I'll end up going for beating the shit out of you. I said get out."

"You don't understand, Jason."

"Don't make me tell you again, Michael."

The fact that Jason was calling me by my name so often clearly demonstrated just how serious he was. I knew he wanted me out of there. His eyes looked toward the door, and I could tell he was wondering if Dad would walk through at any moment, a police officer following close behind. Jason was getting nervous. Now my own tears were flowing, just as the night before.

"I can't live without you," I said. Then I put my hands in my face, just as Jason had done before, and I shamelessly sobbed in front of him. I expected Jason to grab me and throw me out of his place. But he didn't. I felt his hand on my shoulder. Then I felt his massive arms wrap around me as he brought my weeping face close to his chest.

"Come here, kid," he said, and I cried into his shirt for several minutes. To this day, I cherish those last moments I spent with Jason before I would go years without seeing him again. "It's too dangerous. You're tempting me too much. I don't want anything bad to happen to either of us."

I was still crying, still weeping uncontrollably into his shirt. But Jason continued holding me, and for a moment, his compassion for my own fear of losing him exceeded even his own fear of having problems with the law. I told you the night before was the first time I realized I loved him. But that quiet moment feeling his strong arms around me was the first time I realized that he loved me, too.

And we both knew this was goodbye. At least for now.

Jason and I instinctively pulled apart at the same time, and then he took my hand and led me to the door. We stood for a few seconds with our eyes locked.

"You'll know when the time's right, if it ever is," he said. Then he gently shoved me out the door and walked back inside.

He was gone.

Maybe forever, for all I knew.

I stood outside his door for a few minutes, trying to regain my composure before going back to my house. I couldn't walk in with a tearstained face, as my dad would suspect exactly what happened. And he *would* call the cops. He'd make Jason's life a living hell.

I'm often impressed at how little changed that day. I still went to school. Still had homework. Still had friends. And yet there was also some very subtle shift that let me know things would never quite be the same again. It's as if Jason's sudden absence from my life formed a sense of abandonment in me that I couldn't shake even after Jason and I finally reunited years later. My dad could have a field day with emotions like that, and yet it didn't matter. After all, he had caused them.

That was the first time I realized what a funny thing the law is. And how much funnier love is. Neither seemed to make sense. Why would a 15-year-old boy fall in love with a man in his late '20s? Why would the law punish love like that? To this day, I don't know the answer to either of those questions.

But I did know one thing. I hated my father. I hated him worse than anyone. If you had told me then that he and I would one day reconcile and form a powerful father/son relationship that we would both come to cherish more than life itself, I would have laughed in your face and walked away. All I wanted to do in that moment was see my father die. Yes, I hated him that much. I hated him enough to want him to *die*. I had never hated anyone that much before and never have since.

CHAPTER 10

I'm still panting from my recent tickle torture, and Jason approaches me once again and brushes his hand against my cheek before planting a light kiss on my lips. His blue eyes penetrate me to the core as I watch him move around me, taking the rope from my body. God, even feeling my tickle master removing the rope from my skin has an electrifying, erotic aspect to it. Eventually, I feel him moving the rope from my ankles finally letting it fall to the floor.

"I'm not done with you, kid," he says. "Not even close."

I don't respond. I'm excited at more tickling, but I'm also worried. This last tickle torture session in the chair was too intense. Well, almost. But Jason swore he would never hurt me, and even now I believe him.

I hop off the chair, just a little sore from having knelt on it for such a long time, and as I do, the pillow falls to the floor. I start to pick it up, and Jason grabs my wrist and draws me close to him. I look into his eyes and he stares back. I'm lost in the deep sea of blue.

His breathing is heavy, and I know he wants to put me through even more intense tickling, even more torture. And yet, he has an affection for me that perhaps even he doesn't fully understand. He's felt that deep affection since shortly after he met me. And it's only growing stronger now that he's had the opportunity to see me again after so many years.

He pulls back, and he takes off his shirt. God, he's so sexy. I've seen him shirtless before, of course, but I remain amazed at how beautiful he is. Even with heavy pot usage and cigarette smoking, he takes care of his body, working out all the time. His pecs are amazing. He has light tufts of hair on his torso, and it almost completely covers his arms. Even his chest and back are lightly hairy, and I watch him as he walks to the table and pulls another cigarette out of the box, lighting it and moving it between his lips.

"You're a good kid," he says. "Always have been."

I still don't respond. I'm too taken by this sexy, shirtless man smoking a cigarette before me, preparing to put me even further through the rigors of tickle hell.

"Let's go back in the bedroom," he says. "Grab the rope."

I obey, getting all of it and following him to the bedroom. My eyes must surely be filled with excitement at the next adventure to come.

"What do you want me to do?" I ask.

"Get on the bed, but this time on your stomach. Put your head at the foot of the bed. I'll take care of the rest."

Once again, I obey my sexy, shirtless tickle master as I view him with his cigarette hanging out of his mouth. Then he moves behind me, taking a piece of rope – maybe 8 or 10 feet

– and wrapping it around my wrists, getting them secure. Then he grabs my soft, young, bare feet and moves them toward my wrists, bending my knees and taking the rest of the rope to secure them there. Just as before, the feeling of that rope wrapping itself around my bare ankles is erotic as hell. A moment later, I'm in a hogtie the likes of which I might never escape. Even with my arms tied behind me – supposedly protecting my pits from vulnerability – I feel more helpless and exposed than I have yet.

Just as I saw in so many videos years before, Jason crawls onto the bed, and I can almost feel his gaze on my soft, bare feet. It's as if I can feel his eyes studying them, sense the wheels of his mind turning as he considers the perfect way to make those bare feet squirm in ticklish agony. I flex my toes before him as he studies them, wrinkling my bare soles, and I'm staring forward.

As I lie in my bondage, I realize I'm in front of a mirror, and that mirror makes the experience even hotter. It allows me to see myself hogtied, as well as the mischievous expression on Jason's face as he stares at my bare feet. He places his hands over them, and I know this time he doesn't plan to slick them up with oil or lube. This time he plans to dry tickle me. And as I lie there in my hogtie bondage, I wonder if the dry tickling might even be worse than the tickle torture he put me through earlier.

My shoulders ache – but just a little – from the strict hogtie my tickle master has put me in. I wonder if I can take it. And I know the answer. Of course I can! Anything for Jason, my lifelong tickler. I'm young. I'm strong. I can handle this. I can take it. Anything. I think.

Jason starts moving his hands over my bare feet, and instantly I shut my eyes, trying to hold still as I feel those dancing fingers over the soft, vulnerable flesh of my soles. I have determined from looking at fetish porn years before that ticklers like to see a somewhat valiant attempt on the part of the ticklee to remain stoic for as long as possible before releasing their shrieks of tortured laughter. That is certainly the case now. My toes twitch and my vocal cords let out a low moan as Jason runs his fingers over my bare feet, but soon I can bear it no longer. I bury my face in the covers and let out a soft bout of laughter. Then I lift my head and clench my eyes shut, beginning to scream in a ticklish frenzy. I open my eyes and see the sweat forming on my face. My feet are in ticklish agony as Jason unmercifully runs his fingers over them.

Except there's something I hadn't noticed before. I see in the mirror that the same hairbrush Jason tortured me with earlier is sitting next to him. Fuck! I'm not sure if I can take that cruel, stiff-bristled brush on my bare soles yet again. But in this moment, even with my fear of that brush and its devastating ticklish effect on my soles, my main thoughts are on the torture Jason is putting my bare feet through now.

Jason's face is soft. It's actually hot that it's not mean right now. It's almost methodical, like an expert working his craft. His attention is solely on how to create the greatest tickle agony possible for me. Then suddenly, as he's dancing his fingers over my flesh, he begins to dig his fingers into my soles. I've never felt such tickling on my bare feet in my life. The sweat on my body only forms a thicker layer as he scratches deeply into my soles. He's really torturing me now, and I'm still bucking wildly on the bed. I pull against my wrist restraints, trying to see if there's the slightest possibility of escape. I find he's tied me too tightly. My feet are his prisoners. He can torture them ceaselessly, and there's no hope at all of getting away.

"Jason," I say, again in a breathy voice. I'm laughing so hard I can barely speak. I find it's growing more and more difficult to breathe. The torture has become just that. Torture. And I realize this tickling, which was fun before, no longer is. He's scraping my bare feet with his fingernails, and I'm still bucking wildly. My cock is hard underneath me, but there's something about this experience that simply is too much.

"Jason," I say again. My eyes are closed, and I'm having a harder and harder time catching my breath.

"What is it?" he asks, but his voice is cold. The sexual energy of tickling my feet has taken him over. He has objectified me. I'm no longer his friend. I'm no longer the "kid" he loves so much and has spent so many countless hours of fun smoking pot with. I'm simply the object of a gluttonous sexual feast. In this moment, my comfort – even my safety – is secondary in Jason's mind to his own sexual release.

"Please," I say, opening my eyes once again and looking at my frantic face in the mirror. The torture is growing still more intense, and just when I think it can't get any worse, I see him pick up the hairbrush. Instantly, he starts running those stiff bristles over my soles.

"Fuck!" I scream, once again burying my face in the sheets as he tortures my soles. How long does he continue? Five minutes? Six maybe? For all I know, it might be half an hour. Time suddenly has no meaning. When tortured, no moment exists except this one. I stretch my feet out and then flex my toes again. I try crossing my bare feet in my hogtie, but the rope is too secure. I crisscross my soles in an attempt to protect one using the other, hoping to minimize this insane torture as best I can. Once again, Jason grabs my big toes and holds my soles together side by side. He's running the hairbrush over my soles, and there's nothing I can do to stop him. Now there is no escape whatsoever. I must take it no matter how bad it gets. This is true tickle slavery. Jason owns me now. I'm no longer a young man. I'm his property. And he'll do as he wishes with his property. Fuck! It's not supposed to be this way.

I lift my head again, trying with my eyes to catch his gaze in the mirror. But he's completely transfixed with my bare feet. The agony he's causing them is so exciting, he's forgotten I'm a human being. In many ways, he's forgotten how much he loves me. The tickling becomes so aggressive, I wonder how I can ever bear the torture. I think I might die. And yet, I know I won't. I know I'll simply have to take it.

My face is growing red as I steal a quick glance at it from time to time in the mirror. I'm heaving in as much air as my lungs can take. This workout is far more strenuous than any I could undergo at the most intense gym. And yet, he's relentless in tickling my feet.

Then, without a moment's transition or rest, he throws down the hairbrush, leaving my agonized bare feet alone, and moves his fingers in between my arms and my young pits. From the position I'm in, there's no way he can dance his fingers over them. So he places his fingers in between, forcing my arms to trap his fingers there, and he digs deep into my pits. This moment of tickle terror in which I feel the insane pressure of his fingers in my pits is more than I can stand. And yet again, I have no choice. I throw my head back so hard, I'm almost afraid I'll move it out of its socket. I laugh, scream, beg. Surely, Jason knows I can't take much more of this. Surely he knows he's now gone too far. And yet he moves his fingers even *deeper* into my young pits. I look at my hogtied feet in the mirror, feel how tightly I've flexed my young toes, which grow sore from the strict contortions I put them in as a way of dealing with this unbearable tickle stress. And yet, I don't know how else to cope with this unmerciful torture Jason is putting me through.

Does he still love me? Did he ever? Is this all he ever wanted from me? Would he have done this to me when I was 15, only then to kick me out of his house and never see me again once he got what he wanted? All these questions run through my mind as I continue bucking wildly on the bed, barely able to breathe.

"Please Jason!" I scream as loudly as I can. "Please! I can't stand it! I can't!" My eyes are closed as I scream, and still Jason doesn't let up. Not a moment of mercy does he give me. He continues digging his fingers into my soft pits before moving down to my ribs and digging into my flesh there. I try to move my arms as best I can in my bondage, but there's no hope for me to stop Jason from torturing my ribs either. My tickle master has become an uncontrollable demon obsessed with agonizing me, allowing no other thought or desire to enter his mind.

"You'll take it if I say you do," he says.

What? Fuck! How can he be so callous? How can he be so blind to the agony he's inflicting on me. Am I not his friend? His little buddy? Am I not the young man he holds so much affection for and has for years? And yet, he has forgotten. Now I'm just a body to torture as he continues moving his fingers over my ribs and digging into them.

I'm growing dizzy again, and I don't know how much more I can take. Jason starts massaging his cock through his shorts, even as he's tickling the fuck out of me. I'm still moving around on the bed, barely able to speak as I experience this torture. And Jason's huge cock in his pants starts dripping with precum, which seeps through the material. If only he could just finally get off. But he doesn't. Not yet. The torture continues.

"Please Jason! Really, man. Stop. I need a break."

Jason is silent, continuing to torture my ribs, continuing to massage his cock. And suddenly, the precum that had seeped through the material of his pants becomes a glob soaking wet. Jason stops tickling me and lies next to me on the bed. We're both spent.

"Fuck," he manages to say as he lies next to me, looking into my eyes. He's staring at me with a renewed love that left his eyes a while before. But love is not the emotion I feel at this time. I'm pissed.

"You got off. Let me up."

"Okay," he responds nervously, now a look of guilt filling in his eyes as he starts untying my feet and then letting my hands go. I'm still dizzy, but I stand up. Then I walk around, find my shirt and flip flops, and put them on.

"Bye," I say with cold cruelty in my voice.

"Wait. Where are you going?"

I turn around and stare at him, my eyes ablaze. My teeth are gritted as I prepare to speak, but I know I can't fully express to him the anger I feel. I can't do justice to my rage. Anything I say to him will be too good. I spend a few seconds searching for the words, some way to let him know he hurt me, that he took the tickling too far, that he should care about that. That he broke his promise never to hurt me.

He hurt me. He did.

I think, and yet nothing comes to mind. I simply turn and start to walk out. Jason runs ahead of me and stands in my way.

"You have to tell me what's going on," he says.

"It was too much. You knew that, and you did it anyway."

"I'm sorry," he responds, the guilty look only increasing in his eyes. He knows he was wrong. He knows the heat of momentary passion took him over and the tickling was too much for me. He knows tickling me was no longer an expression of love or even affection. It was a way for him to get off and nothing more.

He knows he betrayed me.

"Let me make it up to you," he says.

"There's no way you can do that," I respond, trying to walk around him, but still he blocks me. I'm no longer afraid of him, but he's pissing me off. "Let me by, man."

"I lost you once, Michael. I can't lose you again."

"You just did."

Suddenly, Jason grabs me, and pushes me back. I land on the chair he tickled me on earlier. He holds my shoulders and won't let me up, but it really doesn't matter. I'm not struggling. I've lost the will to fight him. I've lost the will to be defiant or playful or anything else.

"You gonna kill me?"

"Don't be stupid."

He lets go of me, but I remain seated. He's looking out the window, clearly trying to think of a way to keep me here until I forgive him at least enough that I'll come back. Now, outside the heat of passion, he cares about me again. And he cares about my friendship. As I said, he loves me. We love each other. And yet, I have no desire for Jason to hurt me again. Ever.

"You can tickle me," he says.

With those words, time stops. I find even after my hellish ordeal, I'm actually surprised.

Suddenly, the sexual energy that was gone from my body returns. My cock jumps just a little in my shorts, and I'm digging my toes into my flip flops beneath me. Maybe he does need a dose of his own medicine. Maybe he needs to know what it's like to experience that level of tickle torture.

"That's cool," I respond, looking away from him. Still, I don't want to forgive him too soon. I want him to experience the emotional agony of having hurt me, similar to the emotional agony he put me through when he did so. "But not today."

"Please, Michael," he says, coming back to me and moving his lips toward mine. I turn my head away from him, and he pulls back.

"Is that what you wanted?" I ask. "Is that what you get off on? Not just tickling, but really torturing a guy?"

"No," he says, shaking his head. "It was just one time. It'll never happen again."

"It won't if I never let you tickle me again."

Jason gets on his knees in front of me, and he's so sexy as he looks into my face with his big, beautiful, masculine eyes.

"You can tickle me any way you want," he says slowly, carefully enunciating every word, ensuring I know he's dead serious. "You can do anything to me." His eyes moisten, and I feel pity for him, as I'm not used to him showing any kind of strong emotion. "God, I can't lose you again, kid."

For a moment, I think. Then I nod. "I'll tickle you," I respond, standing up. "But tomorrow. Right now, I'm going home."

I start to walk out, and this time Jason lets me by. I look at him as I open the door and walk through it.

"Goodbye Michael," he says. I don't respond. I just leave.

And as I walk back to my house, I realize Dad will be coming home in less than an hour, oblivious to the day's events. Perhaps he'll want to know how everything went, but more than likely he won't even ask. And I'm in no mood to talk about it anyway. I promised Michael I'd tickle him, but even now I'm not sure I'm going to keep that promise. As far as I'm concerned, I'm quite finished with him. The anger I feel at his torturing me even when I clearly told him he was taking it too far still overwhelms me. I'm now even more confused than I was when I arrived at his front door this very morning.

CHAPTER 11

As I said, when I was 15, there was no one I hated more than my dad. He had removed from my life the one man who truly made me happy, and he successfully did so for years. In addition, he had removed my ability to continue looking at porn as well as grounded me and taken my cell phone. To say I was pissed would have been too great an understatement. More accurately, I had a quiet fury buried deep in my spirit that would probably take years to resolve. Dad had not just fucked with my most sacred friendship; he had fucked with my very ability to be happy.

Yes, I liked my cell phone, and it kept me connected to my friends. Not having it wasn't the end of the world, but I used it to check Facebook and chat with friends. I had never used it to look at porn, but I wouldn't be able to now anyway since Dad had sworn to install it with monitoring software. I knew, of course, that if I sneaked and stole my phone back from his bedroom, Dad would find out the next day and demand it back. Still, I was so pissed, I found even the thought of inconveniencing him appealing.

That night, I decided to make my move. I knew he had to be up early for work the next day, whereas being out of school for the summer, I had essentially nothing to do – especially now that I couldn't hang out with Jason in the evenings after he got home. So I sneaked to Dad's room and listened at the door. Yes, he had sensitive ears, but I didn't even care if I got caught. Even if he caught me, the very fact that he knew I was *defying* him would have been appealing. I placed my ear against the door for a moment and listened. Nothing. Not even snoring. That was odd, but it didn't matter. I knew he sometimes slept with the light on (or I always assumed he had from having seen the light coming from under his door late at night), so it didn't surprise me he hadn't turned the lamp off yet. A moment later, I put my hand on the knob and slowly opened it up.

When I got inside, I saw my dad sitting on the bed staring at me like he had come face to face with a demon straight from hell. His face showed the most anguished horror, and I'm sure mine didn't look much better. Dad was completely naked with a laptop on knees. He immediately closed the laptop and put it to the side before throwing the covers over himself.

"What are you doing?" he asked, his voice a mixture of terror and anger.

I stood staring with wide eyes into my dad's face, wondering the same thing about him. Of course, I wasn't that stupid. I really *did* know what he was doing. I just didn't want to think it, even if it was something I had developed a taste for myself.

"It's your mother," he continued, the desperation pouring from his voice. "She's never here. You have to understand, Michael." His eyes weren't moist, but he was getting choked up. Maybe it was the embarrassment of being the hypocrite I now discovered he was. Maybe it was the shame of being caught by his own son watching porn. Maybe it was the guilt at having made me feel so bad about the very thing he was doing himself just days before I was to catch him in the same activity.

I was still silent, still shocked. I just stood there looking at him. I tried to think of something to say, but what could I? And ironically, I was hurt. While I knew Mom was never home, their sex lives never crossed my mind. It never occurred to me that Dad was lonely, that he had the needs of any other man, that Mom wasn't providing those needs because she was always either working or sleeping at the hospital in case of some emergency.

"Hand me that bathrobe," he said, his hands trembling. Immediately, I walked to the chair a few feet from the bed and grabbed it, throwing it over at him. He started to stand up. "Turn around. I don't want you seeing me like this."

I obeyed. What else could I do? I turned and faced the door I had just come through and listened as he threw the covers off and stood up, putting on the bathrobe immediately after.

"Now," he said, and I turned back to face him. "Sit down, Michael."

Dad sat on the bed, and I sat in the chair where I had just grabbed the bathrobe. The shock I felt temporarily made me forget that I hated my old man worse than anyone else in the world. I stared at him with wide eyes. Unsure of what to say. Unsure of how to feel. Unsure of anything. I wondered if my dad felt as terrified walking in on me looking at Internet porn as I felt walking in on him.

"It's a curse, Michael. Our curse. Our whole family has this problem." His eyes were finally starting to grow moist. "I remember when I was younger than you, my own father – who you thankfully never had the chance to meet – started going to visit a lady everyone called Ms. Virginia. I didn't know it at the time, but apparently everyone knew what it meant to go visit Ms. Virginia." Dad was looking past me now. It's like I wasn't even there, like he was speaking to himself or to a ghost only he could see. "My mother knew. Everyone knew. I eventually knew what it meant. It was a source of shame for the whole family." Now my dad turned his head and looked straight into my eyes. "Dad was in his '40s, but Ms. Virginia wasn't much older than you. I don't know how old exactly, but not much older for sure. He did his best to stop. He saw the minister, and they prayed together. He saw a counselor, and that was one of the reasons I wanted to become one myself." He leaned forward, and as he did so, I leaned back a little. I was growing terrified. No one wants to have a conversation like this with his own father.

"Why are you telling me this?"

"Because I don't want you to become what he was. What I am. What Ms. Virginia was. I'll be damned if that's going to happen to you. I know you think I'm a shitty father, and you're right." Dad was looking past me again, clearly unable to look me in the eye as he commented on what he and I both considered his own failures as a father. "But I still have to protect you if I can. I told you I've seen people ruined." He leaned forward a little further, and the intensity increased on his face. "Ruined, Michael. I've nearly been ruined myself. My dad ruined our family. Wrecked it. And all because he couldn't control his urges as a man." Dad moved his feet up and got back on the bed, now resting his head against the headboard. He didn't even take off his bathrobe. He just lay there, looking almost like he was already asleep sitting up. "I'm not going to let that happen to you."

I didn't entirely understand what my dad was saying at the time, but I eventually came to. And in some ways, I eventually came to appreciate his actions as the valiant efforts they were. Perhaps he was trying to be a better father than he had been when I was a young child. Perhaps he was ashamed. Perhaps he just wanted to save me from what he felt had destroyed both himself and his own father. But after he got back on the bed, I remembered what he had done, and my hatred of him returned.

"I don't have to ruin my life. You already have."

Dad shook his head. "You'll understand one day I hope. But for now, I just do the best I can. I put that software on your phone. It's actually blocking software, so it'll keep you from going on porn sites at all. I chose that because I figured you didn't care if I knew what you did. But maybe this will stop you and you won't have to go through all I have." He turned his head and looked over at me, his eyes still as intense as they were before. "I want to help you, Michael. Please let me help you."

"Where's my phone?" My voice was cool and distant.

Dad drew in a deep breath. "Top drawer in the chest of drawers. You'll find it."

I stood and walked to the chest of drawers and pulled out my phone. I turned it on and looked at it. It seemed normal, but I knew he wasn't lying when he said he put blocking software on it. Of course, I planned to try it out, but mainly just to verify what I already knew. I would be unable to access any porn on my phone. But I did see one ray of hope. Dad was softer now. It's like my discovery of his own darkest secret had broken down his barriers. Maybe…

"What about Jason?"

Dad pushed his feet off the bed and jumped up, walking quickly toward me and standing in my face. I was afraid for a moment, as I had never seen him act quite that violently before. I stepped back, and he stood where he was.

"You're not going to be like Ms. Virginia, Michael. Never."

Then he walked back to the bed and got in it, flipping off the lamp as he did so. For several minutes, I stood in the dark. Then I walked out, closing the door behind me. Sneaking into Dad's room had only made things worse. Now my relationship with him would become even weirder and more strained than it already was. Now I would have trouble looking him in the eye. Now I had no hope whatsoever of seeing Jason. And it was all my fault. Fuck!

CHAPTER 12

The stress of experiencing Jason's tickling me going way too far yesterday consumes my thoughts and has all day. So I've broken my own rule.

I smoked pot without him.

I went to Priest's house earlier and had a friend vouch for me. The little man squinted his eyes as he handed me the small bag, taking my crumpled cash in his dirty hand before showing me the door. Now I'm walking up to Jason's house, and I'm stoned as fuck. Jason said I could tickle him, and I'm ready. It's about nine, and I had supper earlier. My belly is satisfied, and my lungs are full of weed. Yes, I'm ready.

I walk into Jason's house and see he's at his kitchen table smoking a cigarette. His eyes aren't bloodshot like mine most likely are, and he looks relaxed as he stares at me. It's almost like he's been expecting me for a few hours. He's wearing his mechanic shirt as always, along with his pants. But my first glance goes to his bare feet under the table.

He smiles. "You ready, kid?"

I continue staring in silence. The pot makes my mind foggy, but I just motion for him to follow as I walk toward the bedroom. He does. He stands up and walks in behind me. I can sense he's standing near me as we walk, his hands at my hips, maybe trying to ensure I don't topple over. I don't know what his problem is. I'm not *that* fucked up, and I intend to prove it to him.

Jason stands near the bed, and I walk up to him. He takes his shirt off and then starts to unbutton his pants, pulling them down. Now, he's stripped down to his boxer briefs and wearing a sexy smile. I'm not buying it. I'm still pissed. I take my hand and shove it into his chest, pushing him back on the bed. My soft attempt at pseudo-violence only excites him more.

"Kinda rough, aren't you?"

"I don't give a fuck."

Jason keeps grinning as he changes his position and lies on the bed the same way I did the first time he tied me yesterday. He's now on his back as he stretches out his arms, his feet lying comfortably at the foot of the bed. I look over and see the same rope he tied me with yesterday. Each piece sits arranged neatly on the floor. I never asked if Jason was a boy scout at one time or where he learned to tie knots the way he did, but rope work just seemed to come naturally to him.

It dawns on me just now that I, on the other hand, have never worked with rope. Years ago I watched a few porn videos, but very few of them actually showed the model being tied up. Most of the models were already tied when the video began. And I never really paid attention to the ones that showed the top tying the bottom, so now I find I'm not entirely sure what to do. Combine that with the pot, and I'm pretty sure I'm completely useless. But I'm determined to tickle Jason. God himself can't stop me. Ignorance of rope and bondage certainly can't.

I pick up the rope, unwind it, and start moving it around the bedframe as I watched Jason do the day before. I bring the two strands next to his wrist. I try to tie a square knot as Jason did, but I can barely even get my hands to move without shaking, and I don't know how tie one anyway. Jason chuckles, and that pisses me off all the more. I throw him a sour look, and he sits up.

"Let me show you," he says. He puts one piece of rope over the other, tying it like someone would a shoelace. Then he doubles that with another tie over done almost exactly the same way. Now I know what to do to this point. Jason lies back, still wearing that grin. "Wrap both pieces around my wrist," he continues. "Move them through the hole there." I try to follow his instructions, and I think I'm doing okay. If I weren't so fucked up, I think I'd do better. But this will work. "Now wrap it around in the other direction and just tie it off. It doesn't have to be perfect."

I do my best. And my pride, coupled with the fact that I'm still pissed at Jason, makes me want to do it perfectly. Still, when I finish tying his right wrist, I notice he would be able to get out of it without the slightest struggle. Fuck!

At least now I have some idea of what I'm doing, though. I walk around to the other side of the bed and repeat the process. I tie his left wrist just as loosely as his right. I'm not happy about the fact that he can easily escape, but I'm too high to care too much. I walk to his feet and get each of them tied, taking a moment to study his soles as I do so. At this point, I realize I've never actually gotten a close look at Jason's feet. They're soft, wide, and meaty. Nothing like the feet I would expect a rugged mechanic to have. I secretly wonder if he takes extra measures to care for them, sneaking to the mall for a pedicure and hoping no one sees him.

A moment later, I have him tied spread eagle, as much at my mercy as I could make him considering my lack of experience with bondage, ready to put him through the rigors of unmerciful tickle torture *at least* to the extent he tortured me last night. I *intend* to take this too far. My cock is growing hard in my pants, and I'm surprised. I always suspected I only wanted to *be* tickled rather than *do* the tickling, but now that I find myself in a position of power, it's exhilarating. I kick off my flip flops and take off my shirt, leaving my shorts on, and crawl onto the bed, straddling Jason's torso. I look into his blue eyes and get lost in them. He's staring back with a look of excitement and bewilderment. Viewing this man's glassy eyes is as exciting to me as it will be to watch him pretend to struggle against my half ass bondage job as I prepare to dig my fingers into his flesh.

As I move my hands toward his sexy, manly pits, my fingers form claws, just as Jason's did yesterday, and his eyes grow wide as he watches. He moves his head from side to side, trying to get a good look at each of my hands as they move closer and closer to his lightly hairy pits, trying to ensure he knows just a second before I plan to begin my attack. There's a look of excitement on his face, but also worry. He knows he took the tickling too far last night, and he knows he's in for hell as I get revenge on him.

I hold my hands still as they hover over his pits, and a sexy layer of perspiration forms on his beautiful, masculine face. His eyes grow wide, and he mouths the word "no," but his playful and mischievous eyes show me he's just as excited about this as I am.

Then I move my hands into his pits, as if thrusting, and he throws his head back and laughs. His hands in the bondage I attempted form fists, and he almost tries to use the strength of his torso to throw me off his body. But I hold fast, bracing myself with my knees as I continue moving my fingers over his flesh, torturing him without mercy just as he tortured me last night.

He moves his head forward again, and he's still laughing, but his eyes are still filled with playfulness and mischief. And love? Is it possible? I stop for a moment, and Jason takes several deep breaths, never removing his gaze from my own. I know the look on my face is serious, even with the weed giving my eyes their current bloodshot appearance. Our communication is silent, and yet it swells with thoughts and feelings moving between us. He shakes his head, and now I move my fingers over his ribs. He continues moving his body, trying to throw me off of him, still forming fists with his hands as he pulls against the restraints from which he could easily escape if he wanted and simply chooses not to.

That's the fascinating thing about Jason's current tickle torture. He doesn't have to take it. I botched his bondage, and he could easily get away. But he doesn't. He takes it. I move my fingers faster, torturing his flesh even harder than before. Now his eyes are closed as the sweat forms an even thicker layer on his forehead.

I stop, and he opens his eyes. I let him think I'm taking a break. Then I immediately start moving my fingers over his ribs again, and once again he struggles in his bondage. Occasionally I turn my head to view his sexy, masculine toes tightly flexed as he uses them as a means of coping with the harsh tickling ordeal I'm subjecting him to.

I move back to his pits, and I notice his pillow is already wet with sweat as I move my fingers even faster over his flesh. He cries out from time to time.

"Michael!" he screams. "Please!" His eyes are closed as he calls out my name, but he immediately opens them and tries to look into mine as best he can under the cruel constraints of the torture. I'm tickling full force now, digging my fingers into his ribs just short of bruising the man who was once my tickle master and is now my tickle slave. This is fun! Fuck, I could do this all night.

Once again, I stop, and Jason is panting in his bondage, looking at me.

"I can't take it, kid," he says between labored breaths.

If he can't take it, then why does he? Why doesn't he pull his hands out of the rope and throw me on the bed, "forcing" me to take the tickle torture he knows he should be rightfully subjecting me to instead of the other way around? The fact that he doesn't try to escape at all tells me my torture has not yet gone far enough.

I crawl off his torso and move further down to the foot of the bed. Now I'm going to attack his bare feet. I look in fascination at his twitching toes as he lifts his head and watches my every move. His hands remain in fists as he braces himself for further torture. The pot has me taken over still. I grab the big toe on his right foot, and I'm not gentle. He winces, but just for a moment. Perhaps not in pain as much as surprise. Then I hold his bare foot in place by grabbing his big toe and move my fingers over his soles. Instantly, his ankle tugs at his bondage. Immediately I know his feet are far more sensitive than his upper body, and I milk that knowledge for all it's worth. I scrape my fingernails over his sole and continue.

His eyes are desperate. They're pleading with me, and I can tell he's struggling. But not with the tickle torture. Of course, the tickling is becoming too much for him. But the fact is he knows he went too far with my own bondage and tickling just last night. He wants to give me this chance at revenge. His truest struggle is to take this insane tickle torture that I know is moving him beyond the brink of insanity without actually pulling his hands from his bondage and putting a stop to it. In his mind – and perhaps in mine, as well – he owes me a debt. He owes me this tickle torture. His fists contracting even more tightly shows me he's using all his willpower to keep his hands in that bondage and take the tickle torture as best he can. The fact that his struggle is as mental as it is physical makes the whole ordeal even hotter. For both of us.

Now I move to his left foot, torturing it as badly as I did his right. But it's not enough. I stop for a moment, once again leaving him panting on the bed, sporting a huge erection in his boxer briefs that I know he'll have to satisfy the moment he finds the first opportunity.

I get up and walk out of the bedroom.

"Where are you going?" he asks, the playful look on his face letting me know he's fully aware of exactly where I'm going. I run into the bathroom and return within 15 seconds. In my hand I hold a hairbrush, the tickler's greatest weapon. Jason is still panting. His face is still sexy. I can tell he's worried, but he's also wearing a serious expression that says he's determined to take the tickle torture to the best of his ability. He wants me to get revenge. He wants to impress me.

He cringes at the thought of losing me again. And this is how he's trying to ensure he won't. He'll take as much tickle torture as I want to give him as long as he can cling to the small hope that I'll never be forced out of his life for yet another period of years. And as these thoughts run through my mind, I wonder how far he wants to take this. All of this.

I place a firm grip on the hairbrush and walk to his right foot. I take my other hand and press it against his toes, pulling taut the flesh on his sole. I look at his face, and he's closed his eyes as he lays his head against the pillow. He's also holding his breath. Feet tickling with a hairbrush might be more than even he can bear. This will be the real test. The hairbrush might break him. And I want to see if I can break him. I *want* to break him. And not just for revenge. I want to break him because I love him. I've admitted I love him before, and I know it makes no sense to want to break a man I love. And yet, this is how I feel. In breaking this man, I can truly express my love for him, possibly even build him back up. Maybe we can both build each other up. All these thoughts flash through my mind at lightning speed over the course of a few seconds as I press my fingers against his toes and rest the hairbrush against his sole.

Then I begin the torture like never before. I scrape the hairbrush over his right sole without mercy. He starts to pull against the rope bondage with all his might, but his ankles really are tied too tightly to escape. He bends his knees slightly as he pulls against the rope, but I just continue moving the hairbrush over his sole without mercy. I scrape and scrape, the flesh on his foot crawling. That sole's flesh wrinkles and flexes and contracts and contorts. His whole body is shaking as I torture his foot. Even his torso is moving back and forth. The young, healthy, masculine laughter coming from his throat excites me all the more and only makes me want to torture him even harder.

"Please! I can't! Michael, I can't stand it!" His words are not mere words; they're cries for mercy. Cries that fall on deaf, if not unwilling, ears. Although he screams them out. My cock grows harder as he calls my name. But I'm relentless. Mercy is the furthest thing from my mind. Perhaps if I weren't as high as I am, I might feel some pity for him. But now all I feel is the rage that comes from the mixture of feelings of betrayal from the previous night as well as the demonic sexual energy running through me and even the love I feel and have always felt for this man. All these thoughts and emotions come to a head as I scrape his sole, listening to the shrieks for mercy like a frenzied Mozart symphony at the climax of a crescendo.

The sweat is running down his face and covers his torso. His eyes turn from wild excitement to pleading and fear. Now I realize *I* have taken the tickling too far. But I don't care. I continue. I want to hear his screaming, his pleading, his tortured cries for mercy. I want to see the desperation in his eyes as I continue moving the hairbrush over his flesh, forcing him to feel every second of ticklish agony.

Am I getting out of control? Maybe. But again, I don't care. I'm torturing him at least as badly as he tortured me last night, if not worse.

"Michael," he says. He almost whispers my name now as the ticklish tears start running down his cheeks. I know the torture is too great for him, and yet he still keeps his hands in the bondage he can surely escape.

And I realize – again – that he must love me.

For even more terrifying than the tickle agony I am putting him through that has gone far beyond what he can bear is the fact that I might fall out of his life again. He will take every bit of the torture I give him. He'll take it as hard and as long as I want. Jason tickled me long and deep yesterday. And now I've tickled him. We've both been tickled by each other.

Tickled hard.

And those two words form the basis of our relationship. The tickling forms our friendship. He wanted it all along. I came to crave it myself. The tickling also makes us lovers. It makes us partners. It forms our spiritual connection. And not just light tickling or playful tickling. But hard tickling. To form the deep, absolutely profound and very complex relationship we have, we had to be tickled by each other. Tickled hard. Yes, that's what had to happen.

I continue moving the hairbrush over his sole. And then I suddenly stop. It's not because I want to. It's because I hear the front door open. I eye Jason and he throws me a worried look. A moment later, Dad walks into the room, and he's holding a gun, pointing it straight at Jason.

"Dad!" I scream.

Instantly, Jason pulls his hands from his bondage and goes to work on his ankles. I approach my dad and try to get the gun from him, but he grabs me and shoves me to the side. He moves toward Jason and points it straight at him.

"Stop," he says, and Jason obeys. He leaves his bare ankles tied and holds up his sweaty, exhausted hands.

"Dad, what are you doing?"

"What are *you* doing?" he screams back, turning a little to the side to face me but leaving the gun pointing straight at Jason's head.

"Please," Jason says. "Please. He's legal. He's legal. I didn't do anything before that."

Dad turns back to Jason, the hate in his eyes more terrifying even than the tickling Jason subjected me to last night.

"I don't care if he's 50. He's not some man whore. You're not doing this to him."

"Dad!" I scream again, and then I hear the gun click. My dad is ready to fire it. My God. I'm convinced Dad will shoot him. He'll kill the man I love.

"Please," Jason repeats, beseeching my dad for his life as frantically as he beseeched me for mercy from the tickling my dad's interruption tore me from. Dad moves closer to Jason.

"Is this what you want from my son? You want to get your rocks off on him with this sick shit?"

Clearly Dad doesn't pay attention to the fact that Jason is the one tied up. But thank God it *was* Jason and not me this time. Had it been me, he would have surely shot Jason on the spot. Dad's eyes are growing moist, and he's breathing harder as he points the gun at Jason.

Slowly, I approach my dad. I wedge myself in between him and Jason, forcing my dad to point the gun at me instead. Immediately he moves the gun away, pointing it at the floor. Now he drops it. Now he kneels to the ground and places his face in his hands, sobbing uncontrollably.

Jason uses this opportunity to continue undoing his ankle bondage while I sit in front of dad. The pot is still running through my body, but I try to pull myself together in this emergency in a moment when my dad has fallen apart.

Dad looks up at me, the despair registering clearly on his face. "What have I done to you, Michael?"

"You didn't do anything. Nothing. You didn't do this."

"I did. I failed. I'm a total fucking failure of a father."

It is in this moment, for the first time, that I realize what I must say to Dad. I have to tell him the truth. I have to tell him what he needs to hear but can't believe. I shake my head just a little, trying to focus my attention on my dad's tormented state.

"I'm not Ms. Virginia."

With those words, Dad begins sobbing again, now lying on the floor in what appears to be a melodramatic expression of his disapproval of my sexual activity with an older man. Except it's *not* melodramatic. It's truly a father despairing that he has failed his son, that his son has turned into the whore his own father visited while raising his family.

"I know you're not," he responds, still crying. Now he sits up, and Jason leans forward on the bed. I look over and quickly shake my head at him, letting him know I'll handle this without his intervention. "But look at you. You're high for Christ's sake. I never taught you that. You're using drugs. You're having this weird sex. Michael, please. Come home. Just come home. We'll get through this if you'll let me try to help you."

Jason starts to stand, but I put my hand up. He stops in his tracks. This one time, I decide I'll try to help my dad.

"Fine," I say. "Let's go home." I look over at Jason and give him a quick nod and a weak smile. I try to let him know in whatever telepathic way I can that everything will be okay. And I hope it will. But I'm not sure. I help my dad up, and as he stands, he also keeps me from falling over in my own intoxicated state. We make our way out the door and walk back to the house. I realize I'm worried about my old man, but I'm actually more worried about Jason. And I'm especially worried about *Jason and me*. I know – or at least suspect – that things between us have become even more serious after tonight's events. I just hope our relationship, or whatever it is we have or this is, can survive after this ordeal.

CHAPTER 13

Dad and I help each other into the house. He looks over at me with a tearstained face, and I can easily tell he's still upset. In some ways, I feel he's more upset than he's ever been. And in this moment – if in no other – I can empathize with my old man in a way his grad school instructors taught him to empathize with his patients. He feels he is a failure as a father. He feels he is a failure as a psychologist. He knows he essentially lost my mom years ago when she completely devoted herself to her work. Now he wonders if he might lose whatever he still thinks he has of me.

He sits down in the living room, and I sit in another chair near him. I try to look into his eyes, but he averts his gaze. The shame has overcome him. Even with all his professional training, he fundamentally believes he's solely responsible for the development of what he considers my bizarre fetish. Finally, when he gets enough courage, he looks into my eyes. I'm already staring at him.

"What do you tell your patients?" I ask him.

"When what?"

"When those CEO's and those men getting ready to get thrown out of their homes come in and say they look at porn.

You told me it ruined them and nearly ruined you. What do you tell them?"

"I…" but Dad's words trail off. Again he looks away from me, and he's clearly trying to hide what he considers his own obvious hypocrisy. Then he looks back, his hands trembling in his lap. "I tell them to find a men's group to talk about it."

"I don't need a men's group. You know that."

Dad nods. "I'm trying to accept that. You didn't get that curse that my own dad and I have. It's hard not to think you have it, too. But you don't have the compulsion that I do. Certainly not what he did." Dad leans forward. "I'm just trying to protect you, Michael. I just want what's best for you. What's best for us. I mean, we're a family. The two of us. You and me. Your mom's never here. It's just us. I wanted…" and his voice trails off again.

"What?"

"I wanted to make a family for both of us. And I couldn't. I wanted to make a household you'd be happy in and proud of. And not only could I not stop you from falling for an older man, I couldn't even stop you from smoking pot. You're way too smart to do something even that benign."

"It's not that big a deal."

"No, it's not. But tying and getting tied is. I take it he's tied you, too?"

Slowly, I nod. I'm silent for a moment. Then I respond. "Yeah."

"What if he had killed you, Michael? What if someone else kills you?"

"He didn't. He saved me. If it weren't for him, I'd be dead."

Dad looks at me again, and his face is pale. His eyes are wide, filled with questions. Filled with confusion. He surely wonders what in the name of God I could possibly mean.

"If Jason hadn't been there for as long as he was, and if I hadn't known on some level I could go back to him when I got old enough, I would have killed myself."

"Why?" Dad asks immediately, almost cutting off my last word.

"Because it's shit living here. Mom's never here. You're not really either. But Jason always was. In a way he still was even when you made me stop seeing him."

Dad lowers his gaze again, and I wonder for a moment if I took my words too far just as Jason took last night's tickle torture.

He looks back up at me. His face is still pale. He's still lost and confused. "Then I'm grateful for him." He nods, almost violently. "Grateful to God for him. If you had killed yourself, I would have killed myself, too. I would have no one. Nothing. That's what would have ruined me completely. It would have finished me off." Dad's looking past me now, his eyes as lost as they were a few years ago the night he told me about his father's affair with Ms. Virginia. "As much as I've studied and learned, I couldn't even give my own son a happy house to grow up in. And people pay me to tell them how to do just that."

Now I feel Dad really is being too hard on himself. After all, for all his mistakes and failures, I know now he really does care and always has. I sit forward, and I realize I'm starting to come down from my high.

"I'm glad you told me everything you did. But I don't know what your problem is with Jason. He's my best friend."

There, I said it. Again Dad looks at me with confusion. I can tell he wonders how I could say such a thing about a man over a decade my senior. And yet it's true. My time together with him, the pot, the tickling, all of it has bonded us in a way many close friends never experience. And as I speak to my dad of my friendship and love for Jason, I'm surer of myself than I have ever been.

"I will learn to like him," Dad says. "It won't be tonight or tomorrow. But I'll try. Because I'll do anything for you. I only want you to be happy. If he makes you happy, then he makes me even happier."

"I hope so," I respond. "I hope you'll give him a chance."

"I will. I'll try. I can at least promise that."

With those words, Dad stands and starts walking upstairs. I'm now alone with my thoughts. And my worry. Last time Dad freaked Jason out, this best friend of mine and I didn't speak for years. I'm not sure I can deal with that again. So I do the one thing I know I must. I walk outside and make my way next door. I have to resolve this somehow. And not tomorrow. Tonight.

CHAPTER 14

As always, I walk unannounced into Jason's house and find him sitting at the kitchen table, having smoked perhaps a dozen cigarettes since I left his house earlier. He wears a despondent look on his face. He's still shirtless and barefoot, but he's thrown on a pair of pants. His eyes are blank as they stare forward. It's as if he doesn't even realize I'm there. I sit in front of him, but still he doesn't acknowledge my presence. He just continues staring forward, puffing on the cigarette from time to time, clearly shaken by the evening's events.

And I realize now that I did what I said I would. I tickled him without mercy. True, he could have escaped, but maybe he felt I was just as excessive in tickling him as he had been in tickling me. And while tickling him without a modicum of mercy was my intention when I was still high, I now suddenly feel differently. I move my hand forward and snap my fingers in front of his face. He blinks and looks into my eyes.

"Hey," I say.

"You're back," he says, moving the cigarette to his lips.

"Yeah."

"Why'd you come back?"

Now I'm the one who looks away. "You know I had to."

The smoke comes out of Jason's mouth and he puts the butt out in the ashtray sitting in front of him.

"No you didn't."

I lean forward, and Jason is still looking directly into my eyes. "Don't leave me again, Jason. You can't."

Jason stands up and faces away from me. Then he turns back, his eyes ablaze with hurt or anger or some emotion I don't recognize and perhaps has no name. "It's not that, kid. Your dad's right. What I did with you was wrong. Or not what I did, but what I felt. I'm sick, you know."

"Fuck that shit."

"It's true," Jason says, sitting down again, but this time in the chair right next to me. "And it's wrong. I've loved you since the first time I tickled you. And not yesterday morning. But when I had your feet tied on my lap a few years ago. That's wrong. It's just fucking wrong, Michael. I'm a sick man."

"It's not that simple."

"In the eyes of the law it is. In the eyes of most people it is. I felt something for you I wasn't allowed to." Jason sits back, moving his whole body in the other direction, as if cowering away from a snake that might strike him at any moment. "And I still feel that way."

"That's okay."

"It's not, Michael." Jason's blue eyes now move back in alignment with my own. "Jesus."

"What's wrong?"

"If I hadn't kicked you out that day, I don't know what I would have done. I might have tied you up when you were still 15. I just don't know. Jesus."

"But you didn't."

Jason's face suddenly clouds, and a look of severity covers it. It is grave, serious, somber. "I swore I would never hurt you, and I meant it. Then I broke that pledge. You and I both know that. I can never take that back."

"I got you back, man. I tickled you real hard a little while ago."

"I know. And I'm glad. I wanted you to. Hell, I want you to do it again." Once again, Jason averts his gaze. His admission that he just can't get enough is too much for him even now. God, he still loves me. And I still love him. After all that's happened, our love is indestructible.

I smile as best I can during this tense conversation. "And I want you to. Dad and I talked. It's gonna be okay. He's okay with you now. At least, he will be."

"How do you stand it there, Michael?"

"I don't know." Now I'm looking away from *him*. How *do* I stand it there? Even now that Dad and I reconciled and will hopefully continue to grow in our father/son relationship, how did I ever stand living in a house with a distant father and an absent mother? How can I stand it now? I look back at Jason, hoping what I'm feeling will pour forth in words, and yet it's so hard to think of just the right thing to say. "I have to get out of there. I have to go somewhere else."

"I can't lose you again, kid." Jason stands and towers over to me, looking down into my eyes. And I look up into his. It's as if he's asserting his authority over me, and yet also protecting me, as well as himself, from the emotional agony of our renewed separation. If he doesn't block my exit, he at least plans to act like he will. But I don't resist. I sit in silence, allowing myself to get lost in the deep blue of his eyes. Finally, I speak.

"What can I do then?" I ask, a glimmer of hope suddenly coming into my mind as I pray to God or Whoever that Jason will say the words or ask the question or make the request that I have wanted for so long.

"You'll come live with me, kid. We'll figure this out. Together."

And so the words poured forth. I heard what he had to say, and I'm glad. A quiet contentment returns to my spirit as I realize that I at least have the option of living with the man I have loved for years and yet that laws and parents and society forbade.

"Yes," I say. And that one word is all I have to say.

But of course, I have questions. A million. What will our relationship be? How will it work? Will he be just another older guy telling me what to do? Will he tickle me every night? Will we eventually come to have sex?

I don't know the answers to any of these questions, and yet I know I have to try. I have to allow myself to explore adulthood, and this is my first step. With that one word – that yes – I allow myself to go into uncharted territory and put myself into a situation whose result I don't yet know. But yes, I will try. Jason and I will both try. We will. Together.

CHAPTER 15

It takes less than a week to get my stuff packed, and the following weekend my dad and I start moving my things over to Jason's house. Of course, Jason helps. He's prepared a lot of room for me, as his house isn't the biggest. It's actually much smaller than my parents'. But then, I guess you would expect a single mechanic to live in a smaller place than a surgeon and a psychologist. I decide not to even take my furniture with me. I just grab all the things I care about and shove them in a few boxes. The whole process only takes a few days.

"Glad you didn't go too far," my dad says as he brings the last box into my new home. His eyes are a little moist, but I suppose that's to be expected. I've always heard that when the kids leave the house, the parents often have a long crying spell, though I wouldn't have expected that to start until after my dad was alone again. And yet, I also know he's not truly alone. In many ways, he's not nearly as alone as he's been for the last few years. True, my mom will continue her work, even to the extent that she never showed up in this story. But it's not like I moved across the country. I'm right next door.

"Well," I say, trying to think of any response at all to Dad's sentimental statement. "In a way, I've never been closer." And in this moment, I realize those are the perfect words. Nothing I could have said would have made him feel any better. He nods and approaches me, taking me in his arms. At first, the embrace shocks me. This is neither Christmas nor a funeral, and yet slowly I reach up and wrap my own arms around my dad's body, as well. I can't yet tell if he's crying, and I look over at Jason, who's trying not to look over at us. A moment later, Dad pulls away. He is not crying, but he has a look of pride in his eyes.

"You're a man now," he says. "In every sense of the word."

"I hope I'm ready for this."

"You are," my dad responds, giving me one more quick embrace before pulling away. "Well," he says, starting to move toward the door. "I think I'll let you two get settled." Of course, now he's going home to cry. That's why he's in such a hurry to leave. Maybe my dad is more melodramatic than I ever thought, after all.

"Okay," I say, watching as he walks toward the door. Now he's gone and is making his way back toward his home and my former home. It's a bittersweet moment. Of course, it *will* take him time to get used to Jason. And considering my dad's behavior a few days ago, it's amazing to me that Jason allowed me to move in at all. And yet he has invited me to do so with open arms. Now we begin our lives together.

When my dad walks out, I turn to Jason, who lunges for me. I'm shocked, but only for a moment.

"What are you doing?" I ask, but he grabs me and practically picks me up and carries me to the bedroom.

"Did you think you were gonna get out of ever getting tickled again just 'cause you moved in with me, kid?"

"No," I say. I lose my flip flops in the process of getting to the bedroom, and a moment later, I peel off my shirt. Jason also gets his shirt off, but he leaves his pants on. He kicks his own flip flops off, and he kneels before me and starts to unbutton my pants, pulling them down but leaving on my boxer briefs.

"Get on the bed, but this time get on your stomach," he says. His voice is soft and breathy. His respirations are heavy, and I can tell he wants this just as badly as I do. "I'm gonna tie you just like you tied me, but on your stomach."

I grin and obey. A moment later, I feel the rope wrapping around my wrists before he goes down to my feet and starts wrapping it around my bare ankles. Now I'm tied on the bed with my arms stretched out to the side and my feet at the corners at the foot of the bed. I close my eyes, waiting for Jason to start ravaging my body with the merciless tickle torture I know he's so capable of. But instead, I feel his hand brush against my cheek. He moves it across my face, and I open my eyes to find him sitting right next to me.

"You're not gonna tickle me?" I ask.

"Sure I am. I'm just not gonna hurt you this time. Not now or ever."

I look up at him and smile, and I can tell by his expression that it's true. Now that he's experienced what it is to tickle me too hard and to be tickled too hard, we both know neither of us will ever do anything like that again.

Jason reaches over and slaps my ass, then gets on top of me, straddling me. I can feel his cock rubbing against my back through his pants as his breath gets even heavier. Now I feel his hands against my ribs. For a moment, he just leaves them there. I close my eyes, waiting for the imminent tickle torture to come. Soon he lightly starts dancing his fingers over my ribs. I buck wildly on the bed, laughing as he moves his fingers up to my young pits. The sweat forms on my body, as it always does during intense tickle torture. He's really tickling me, but just for a moment. Then he stops, and I'm breathless. My eyes are wide as I wait for more.

"I'm never gonna hurt you again, kid. Never," he says, once again dancing his fingers over my pits. I move around on the bed again, easily releasing my laughter. And it's getting louder, but he really doesn't take it too far this time. "Just wait till I get to your feet," he says as I pretend to try to escape his bondage and tickle torture. But in reality I have no desire whatsoever to escape. I only want to be tickled like this long into the night, and I'm sure that's exactly what Jason plans to do. I'll be tickled well into the early hours of the morning. Tickled hard. And I know this time I can take it. I know this time, Jason won't take it too far.

And as I lie here taking my next bout of tickle torture, I have no idea what the future holds for Jason and me. I only hope we make it, that we form a successful life together. A life of love. A life of playful and erotic tickling. A life in all its beauty and ugliness. I want that for both of us.

And as Jason moves down toward my feet during a brief break as he prepares to ravage me there, I pray to God or Whoever that this is not the only night he'll tickle me, but that there will be many many nights of insane tickle torture that go long into the night and well into the early morning hours. I pray this is only one of them. One of many. One of thousands.

And I wonder and hope and pray, as I'm waiting for the tickling to continue, that perhaps the storybooks really are right. Maybe everything does turn out okay. Maybe a couple really can live happily ever after.

THE END

A NOTE FROM A FELLOW MALE TICKLING AUTHOR JERRY B

I felt honored when Adam Small asked me to write some comments for his latest tickle fetish story, *Tickled Hard*. The world of fetish and kink literature has changed so much since I began exploring it for myself in the very early 1990's. It is not that stories were impossible to find, but they were rare as hen's teeth. I had always been turned on by men's feet and tickling but as I approached 30 it started to become an obsession for me. I haunted adult book stores and always gravitated towards anthologies like *Hand Jobs* where, if I was lucky, there would be a mention of foot play or bondage, never tickling. I felt lonely, as if I were the only man in the world who was turned on by such a playful and devilish act. What was wrong with me?

One day I had an epiphany. While thumbing through an anthology of erotica, I ran across an article about a video producer named Bob Jones who was making male tickling fetish videos. I can't tell you how excited it made me feel to discover that I was not alone. There were other men out there who were turned on by the same things. I bought the magazine and then ran to a video store and managed to find a few of his videos. The quality was poor, but in spite of that, I probably came at least four times that evening.

We take so much for granted today, but only 19 or 20 years ago the internet barely existed. Connecting with men who shared my fetish felt nearly impossible at first. But there was chat, and chat rooms sprang up for men who had foot fetishes, and soon I was connected to a few men who shared my obsession. I found out that there was actually a national list of guys who got together for tickle play. Whenever they traveled they could locate someone on the list and try to connect with them. By today's standards it was relatively primitive, done by telephone or e-mail or even snail mail. I never added my name to the list but I did meet some wonderful men who showed me the ropes, in all senses of the word.

It was this same group of men who began writing tickle fetish stories and exchanging them. Not everyone could travel easily, and a list of a few hundred tickle fetishists was not a very big pool to choose from. Even in a city like San Francisco, there were only a handful of guys on the list. But stories could be published and exchanged, kept and re-read. Someone put out *Tickle Master* magazine that was very much like a college publication. There was a popular bondage magazine called *Bound and Gagged* that specialized in true stories. I still treasure my collection of those magazines though I hardly ever read them these days. Quite a few tickle fetish stories made it into *Bound and Gagged*.

The watershed came when "Jack" put up what is still considered the definitive male tickle fetish story website sometime around 2000. *Jack's Male Tickling Rack* gathered many of the stories that had circulated for years. He encouraged guys to write new stories that they could post to a message board, and he accepted new submissions for the permanent collection. The old stories got a little polish to clean up spelling and grammar, but otherwise the stories were completely as the author wrote them. Jack was a prolific writer, but the list of authors included guys like Blithwulf, CatInHat, Dtuc, Eddie, FingrFethr, Glaucon, Huck, Keith Steeclif, Ratty, Scooter McGraw and many others who contributed hundreds of stories.

I was inspired from reading the works of all of those talented writers. Starting around 2000 I began contributing stories to the Internet, as well. I wrote "The Pizza Man", described a "James Bond Interrogation," and wrote a personal experience about "The Birthday Present", among other short stories. Of course I jacked off to the stories on *Jack's Rack*, but they also fired up my sexual imagination. The stories gave me ideas for tickling and cum control scenes, and they also did something very special for me. They made me feel as though I belonged to a sort of online community of guys who shared my kinks. I was no longer alone, and I wanted to contribute in my own way to the world of male/male tickling.

There is so much more content available on the Net than there was back then. I used to wait for weeks just to see a new photograph or video clip. Now new visual material gets released nearly every day. But good stories are still at a premium. Although a few sites keep libraries of stories, the volume of new material is low and the quality can be lacking. That is why I am excited that Adam Small is publishing new male/male tickle fetish material. A good story is often better than a video. You can be a character in the story in your own mind. You can imagine the type of people you want in the various roles. An author like Adam is like a good tickler who puts you through your paces and leaves you breathless, happy, and turned on. I am always ready to go along for the ride, to see where the story takes me, and to feel like I am with a fellow fetishist.

I'll be publishing my own first tickling novella soon, thanks in good part to the encouragement I have received from Adam. I always want to be a contributor to our little kink community. But I can never be a prolific writer and so I will always appreciate and encourage men like Adam Small to write more stories and take us all on a sexy ticklish journey.

JerryB

MEET ADAM SMALL

Adam Small is a tickling and male foot fetishist that loves writing erotic fiction. He also enjoys real time tickling and bondage play with attractive guys between the ages of 18 and 45. One of his favorite forms of bondage is the hogtie, as you can tell. He also enjoys tying guys spread eagle, and he enjoys chair ties and feet suspension. In addition to tickle torture, Adam enjoys all forms of bondage, light bastinado, and role play, as well as good, old fashioned gay sex. Adam is a top in all regards.

Adam Small lives in Tennessee. He was born in the summer of 1978, so you can calculate his age. If you're interested in meeting for tickle play, you can email him at **adam@maletickling.info**. Even if there is no tickling or bondage, Adam loves to get email, love mail, hate mail, etc.

Please email Adam today and let him know what you thought of the story, as well as any ideas you have for future stories. He'll respond as soon as he possibly can.

THANK YOU FOR READING!!! I HOPE YOU ENJOYED READING THIS WORK AS MUCH AS I ENJOYED WRITING IT FOR YOU!!!

Made in the USA
Monee, IL
21 April 2020